SO-BAG-218

CHILDREN'S LIT.

BETHANCOURT

Doris Fein: Phantom
of the casino

DATE DUE			
NOV ...			

PZ
7
.B562

Doris Fein: Phantom of the Casino

T. Ernesto Bethancourt

Holiday House/New York

FOR PHIL HARRIS,
jazzman, gentleman, judge of fine whiskey
and purebred horses,
with thanks for his technical advice.

Library of Congress Cataloging in Publication Data
Bethancourt, T   Ernesto.
  Doris Fein—phantom of the casino.

  SUMMARY: Doris experiences romance, adventure, and
excitement as she investigates a conspiracy directed
against the tourists at the casino of Santa Catarina
Island.
  [1. Mystery and detective stories] I. Title.
PZ7.B46627Dor   [Fic]   80-8814

ISBN 0-8234-0391-2

Contents

The figure moved in a crab-like fashion through the shadows and darkness beneath the fifty-year-old building. Above, in the Casino Ballroom, a band played; people danced, unaware.

The shadowy form emitted a dry chuckle as it dragged the burlap sack of high explosives to its resting place alongside one of the huge concrete piers that supported the building above. In a few minutes, the deadly contents of the sack had been placed alongside similar bundles. As the dim shape connected the electrical wiring that led to other carefully placed charges, it began to hum along with the music that filtered down to the depths of the Casino's catacomb-like foundations.

"'I'm always chasing rainbows,'" the shadowed form sang. "'Watching clouds drifting by. My dreams are just like all my schemes. Ending in the sky. . . .'"

Here, the dimly seen shape broke off singing and laughed aloud.

"Sky-high," it added, giggling. "Sky-high . . ."

1/Open Wide

"Open wider, Doris," said my Uncle Saul. "I think I see a little spot there that could use some work."

As he began to pick and poke at a back molar, my Uncle Saul began to sing "La Donna È Mobile" from *Rigoletto*. Uncle Saul has a beautiful tenor voice, and his passion is grand opera. I don't know if he usually serenades his dental patients with excerpts from Verdi but, being his niece, I got the full treatment. Maybe he does sing for all his patients. When you think of it, would you tell a dentist who's got you in a chair that his singing bothers you? I've heard of captive audiences but, when your dentist sings, you *have* to listen.

"Aha!" Uncle Saul said, abandoning Verdi for the moment. "A teeny gumline cavity there, Doris! Only take me a second . . ." He reached for the high-speed drill and, as the drill bit whined into high frequencies, launched into *"Che Gelida Manina"* from *La Bohème*. In a few seconds, the offending spot had been excavated and filled.

7

"There you are, sweetie," he said, smiling. "Good as new. Not a bad checkup. But you missed two fluoride treatments this summer, you know. You have the Fein family curse: soft teeth. You can't skip such things, hon."

"Sorry, Uncle Saul," I said. "But you know I was in Europe this summer. I didn't have the time. Or the chance, even if I'd had the time. It was very hectic."

"You must make time for your teeth. Remember what I told you when you were only twelve?"

"I know, Uncle Saul," I said patiently, and recited, "Always be true to your teeth . . ."

"And they'll never be false to you," we concluded in chorus. My uncle is big on dental humor, you see. But I do have very good teeth because of him.

What I couldn't tell Uncle Saul was the reason I didn't have time for a dental fluoride treatment in Europe. I was too busy being kidnapped and chased halfway across the continent by a group of international criminals intent on killing me!

I should explain. I'm a spy. That's right, a cloak-and-dagger type. Twice now I've acted as an agent for the I.G.O., the secret government agency that functions along the lines of the C.I.A., but more secretive. I can hear you saying, That's ridiculous. How can an eighteen-year-old girl from a small town in Southern California be an international secret agent? The answer is, not very effectively, but I'm getting better all the time.

My European adventure was my second assignment. Before that, I had acted as a decoy for terrorists who were after my Aunt Lois's husband, Claude Bernard.

He's Economic Attaché to the U.N. for the African nation of Dakama.

The best thing that came out of the whole scary mix-up was that I met one of the most fascinating and handsome men I've ever known. His name is Carl Suzuki.

Then, he had been a detective on the New York City police force. He was also studying law at night. Before the Dakaman adventure was over, Carl and I became *very* close. But not close enough, darnit! The whole relationship was almost wiped out when Larry Small, my childhood sweetheart, showed up in New York concerned for my safety.

I don't know what Larry told Carl about our relationship, but it sure cooled off the romance. Carl is very hip, but being a Sansei Japanese American (the Sansei are third-generation Americans), he can sometimes turn so honorable and ethical, I could kick him in the seat of the pants.

Anyhow, Larry went back to California, but the damage was done.

Until yesterday's mail brought a letter from him, I hadn't heard from Carl Suzuki in over six months. But I had been very busy myself. I had just begun my freshman year at the University of California at Irvine, and was adjusting to college life. Socially, not scholastically, I might add. I graduated from my hometown high school in Santa Amelia, California, with highest honors. Tops in my class, valedictorian: the whole enchilada.

The social life was something else again. I should explain that I am not your typical Southern California beauty. I'm not tall, blond, willowy, and blue-eyed. I look nothing like a Barbie doll. But that's the standard of beauty out here. The guys look about the same, or like Barbie's friend, Ken. Half of them look as though they were born with surfboards under their arms.

I am five feet, four inches tall and, depending upon my self-discipline, either a teensy bit, or a whole lot, overweight. Uncle Saul calls soft teeth the Fein family curse. It isn't; the Fein family curse is good cooking. He's a sterling example, himself. Except for the fact that at age forty two, he's almost completely bald, he looks like a Jewish Luciano Pavaratti. That big.

I used to be very heavy too. But after a long session with my mom, who used to be a nurse, and some counseling, I discovered that I ate out of loneliness, not true hunger. Since then, I have stopped buying dresses in half sizes, something I did from age thirteen to seventeen. But I'm afraid I'll never look like a ballerina. A sylph, I'm not. Grandma Fein says that I'm *zoftig*, which is a nice Jewish way of saying voluptuous.

My hair is medium brown and in summer is sunstreaked. My eyes are hazel green and, thanks to my Uncle Saul, my teeth are beautiful. My best feature, really.

"Okay, sweetie," said Uncle Saul cheerily. "All done. Rinse."

I obligingly rinsed and spat while Uncle Saul busied himself setting up his instruments for his next patient. As he did, he began to sing "Vesti La Giubba" from *I Pagliacci.* At top volume. Fortunately, like most dentists' operating rooms, there was heavy soundproofing. I got up to go.

"See you at dinner tonight?" he asked, interrupting his vocalizing.

"I'll be there for sure," I said, "but I might be a little late. I have to pick up a friend at Los Angeles International Airport at four thirty. If we get caught in the rush, it may take some time."

"Is that the Japanese fellow?" Uncle Saul asked.

"Uh-huh. He's flying in from New York."

"Hope his arms don't get too tired," Uncle Saul said. "It's a long flight!" He laughed. Uncle Saul's jokes are on a par with his dental humor, I'm afraid. But he is a lovely, gentle man, for all his size.

You'd think from his appearance he'd be someone who broke buildings with his bare hands. He's six feet two and weighs somewhere in the neighborhood of a Rams lineman. And he's an extremely hairy man, except for his head. I sometimes think that it's an unwritten law that all dentists and salad chefs must be as furry as the bears in Yellowstone Park.

When you see him next to my dad, you'd maybe think they were related, but only distantly. Dad is a bit under six feet, of medium athletic build, with a full head of hair, like Grandpa Fein. But he and Dad are very close. We have dinner with Uncle Saul and his wife Cecile twice a month. We usually eat at our house. Cecile used to be a figure skater with Ice Follies, and as a cook, she could screw up cornflakes.

Mom is a great cook, though. I know. I carried around the mute testimonial to her cooking for years. But although she and Dad both eat like lumberjacks, neither of them ever seems to gain an ounce. There are only two heavyweights in our family since I retired from marathon eating: Uncle Saul and Grandma Fein.

I got a kiss on the cheek and a bear hug from Uncle

Saul and left the Santa Amelia professional building. I looked up at the early April sky and debated putting the top down on the Flying Gumdrop. That's my Triumph sports car. I got it from my folks as a seventeenth birthday present. It's a lovely car and looks like it's going a hundred miles an hour even when it's standing still. When I first saw it, and the bright green color it was painted, I said, "It looks like a flying gumdrop!" And that's how I gave it the name.

Now, I don't want you to think that I'm some kind of spoiled brat who has gifts lavished upon her by rich parents. My dad is an ophthamologist, and my mom was his nurse for years. To get my car, I worked as a receptionist for Dad after school and during the summer for over a year. Dad believes that a young person should appreciate the value of a dollar. I agree.

I also think that the eighteen months or so I spent dealing with patients and the public in general was a great help to me in life. I had been quite shy and self-conscious about my weight. On top of that, I had a mouthful of orthodontic hardware and blotchy skin from my over-rich diet. But it all seemed to come together during my junior and senior years at Santa Amelia High. I got the job of reporter on the school paper, *The Blade,* and came to have a rewarding relationship with Larry Small, who was editor of the paper.

Deciding that the sky didn't look that promising, I left the top up on the Flying Gumdrop. I started her up, snicked her into gear, and pulled out of the lot. In a few minutes, I was buzzing down the road to Los Angeles International Airport, or LAX, as we seasoned travelers call it. As I did, I thought about the letter I'd received from Carl Suzuki.

He apologized for his silence over the past months. He explained that he'd been cramming for the New York bar examination. But now, he'd been passed through and, to top it all, had been appointed an assistant district attorney in New York. That sounds impressive, but as Carl explained, it's simply a swell title for an awful lot of unglamorous donkey work. He wasn't due to commence his duties with the D.A.'s office in New York for another two weeks. In the meantime, he was coming out to California.

I'd half entertained the notion that he was coming out especially to see me. But he also said in his letter that his uncle, who lived in Los Angeles, was ill; perhaps dying. As Carl's dad is not in very good health either, Carl was to go as his father's emissary. Like I said, the Japanese Americans take family very seriously. And they can be awfully formal about it too.

I thought back on the last paragraph of Carl's letter. *Once I have this family matter taken care of, you and I must have a long talk, Doris,* it had said. *I want to discuss both our futures. I can't wait to see you. I've been practicing my pool shooting, and this time, you won't stand a chance!*

I had to smile at the pool reference. When Carl and I met, one of the things we discovered we had in common was shooting pool. My dad bought a pool table for our family room years ago. He loves the game. But Mom couldn't care less about it. Lacking a partner, Dad taught me the game. I'm quite good, really. The first time Carl and I played, I beat him two out of five games. And he was using his own custom cue stick too.

The sign for the turnoff came up, and I began snaking through traffic to the LAX exit. I put the Gumdrop in a metered space and made my way to the air terminal marked Domestic Arrivals. It's always jammed at LAX. The city fathers keep saying that we need another major airport in the Los Angeles area. Trouble is, no one wants jet planes in his backyard, and they can't find anywhere to build a new airport.

I checked the video repeaters with flight information for Carl's arrival time. The T.V. monitor said that the flight would be fifteen minutes late. I was a half hour early as it was. I looked through the various gift shops, resisted the temptation to investigate any of the restaurants, and did some people watching.

As the time for Carl's arrival neared, I went to the numbered gate at which his plane would be unloading. I saw a number of Orientals waiting, I guess for the same flight. I couldn't help but wonder if any of them were Japanese, or even relatives of Carl's. But then I recalled that outside of his sick uncle, Carl's only other relative out here was his cousin Alvin. And nobody had heard from Alvin in ages. He didn't even know that his father, Carl's uncle, was sick. Evidently, all Japanese Americans weren't as family conscious as Carl.

The huge 747 pulled up to the unloading gate, the automatic umbilicus on wheels that was the passenger ramp swung into place, and the people aboard began to enter the terminal. They all wore that same smile of relief that air passengers wear after completing a successful flight. Come to think of it, who'd smile over an *un*successful one? Wouldn't you know that Carl was among the very last to deplane?

He was wearing a three-piece suit, blue, with a crimson tie. He had a topcoat over his arm, and an attaché case in his other hand. Carl is tall for a Japanese: six feet and perfectly proportioned. His face reminds you of a typical, clean-cut Ivy Leaguer's until you notice that his eyes slant and his cheekbones are too high for a suburban country club.

"Carl!" I called. "Over here!"

He spotted me at once and made his way through the people who inevitably embrace each other at the very exit of the boarding ramp, blocking the exits of others behind them. I was about to comment on how good he looked when, in a second, he dropped both attaché case and topcoat and planted a huge kiss on my lips! If the bystanders gaped at racially mixed necking in the terminal, I couldn't say. I always close my eyes when I kiss. But I don't close my mind. All through the big wet one, I kept thinking of that last paragraph in Carl's letter. The part where he said, I want to discuss both our futures.

I had a momentary sinking feeling in my stomach. I was beginning to understand what Carl had meant. And though I'm very attracted to him—just as much as I was in New York—what he seemed to have on his mind was a *very* serious relationship. One I might not be ready for. But just then, his arms were *very* cozy. I decided to wait and see. Sooner or later, he'd come up for air and start talking.

2/You Can't Get a Sword
   in My Trunk

We made our way past the Hare Krishnas begging for contributions, walked almost two blocks on a moving beltway that wasn't moving, and finally got to the baggage claim, where we waited for fifteen minutes until the luggage conveyer belt regurgitated Carl's bags down a rubber-belted throat to a carrousel display of Gucci through Sear's luggage.

As the bags went by looking like some strange vinyl-and-leather smorgasboard, Carl picked out two large suitcases. I was ready to go, but evidently Carl had still more property to claim. After almost all the assorted carry-off bags had come down the chute, Carl's last item arrived.

It looked like a gift-wrapped curtain rod in a sturdy fiberboard carrying case. I didn't ask what it was, but I already knew that, whatever it was, it couldn't fit into the trunk of the Flying Gumdrop. Seeing Carl had his hands full, I put the long object under my arm and took the attaché case he had carried off the plane. Carl picked up the two large suitcases and, laden like camels bound for Samarkand, we angled our way through the terminal doors.

"What is this I'm carrying?" I said over my shoulder, leading the way to my car.

"It's a sword," Carl said.

"Stop fooling around with the skycap," I said. "What is it really? A painting rolled up? Maybe a Japanese scroll?"

"Wouldn't kid you for the world, Doris. It's a sword. An antique."

I stopped in front of the Gumdrop and said, "I don't care if it's a matched set of pool cues. You can see the problem we've got." I indicated the trunk of my sports car and shrugged. Not easy to do without dropping your sword.

"Maybe I should get a taxi," Carl said.

"Don't be silly," I said hurriedly. "New York cabs are dirt cheap next to Los Angeles cabs. That's if you can find one."

"At an airport, that's not too hard," Carl said.

"Carl Suzuki, I didn't drive thirty-five miles to this airport only to see you off in a cab!" I said indignantly. "I can put the top down on the car. That way there'll be room for your . . . sword."

We set down the luggage and for a few minutes wrestled with taking the top down. When I got my owners manual for the Gumdrop, it consistently referred to the removable hardtop as a "one-man top." Outside of the sexist connotation of its title, the "one man" involved had to be Arnold Schwartzenegger.

I was about to get behind the wheel, when I noticed the expression on Carl's face. He was looking at the Gumdrop the way my alter ego, Petunia, would eye a hot fudge sundae. I suddenly understood.

Carl is a New Yorker. They never have cars or drive anywhere. In that city, a car is truly a luxury. My sports car was actually exotic to him. I couldn't help but wonder what he'd think of the many Alfas, Mercedes, and Rolls-Royces one sees on Southern California freeways.

"Want to drive?" I asked, holding out the keys. He grinned like a little boy.

I guided Carl through the maze of side roads and turnoffs, to the freeway that would bring us south to Santa Amelia.

I gave directions once we exited from the freeway. I guess I wanted Carl to see bustling, beautiful downtown Santa Amelia.

"That's the Pacific Hospital over there," I said. "Larry Small's mom works there." Carl nodded. "And that's *The Register,* the newspaper that Harry Grubb owns . . ."

Harry Grubb is our local millionaire, though you wouldn't know it from the way he acts. Harry was a crime reporter on the *Chicago Tribune* for most of his adult life. (He's close to eighty now.) But, a number of years ago, he married a wealthy widow in Chicago. After one year of marriage, the lady died, leaving Harry millions. He came to Santa Amelia to retire from Illinois winters and to write his memoirs.

But he soon discovered that the inactivity was driving him around the bend. He then bought the local newspaper, just so he could hire himself as a crime reporter. Considering how little happens in Santa Amelia, the joke was on Harry. In a sense, he's still semi-retired.

Though I don't think it was a great thing he did, it was Harry who loaned Larry Small the money for air fare to New York. Then, snoop that he is, Harry came along with Larry to check up on me and my ill-fated romance with Carl. In no time at all, Harry Grubb and Carl became thick as a Baskin-Robbins milkshake. I guess it was Carl's police background.

"Turn left at the next signal," I told Carl. I'd been so lost in thought that I'd almost missed my own turnoff. It was a close, tight turn, and the long parcel containing the "sword" slid over and rapped me sharply on the shoulder.

We went a few more blocks, made another turn, and pulled up in front of my house. Carl got out immediately and headed for my side. He was going to open the door for me, I'm sure. I quickly snaked out of the car before he could. Not that I don't appreciate the intent of men who do such things; I do. But the idea that a woman can't get in and out of a car unassisted is absurd. And I haven't had trouble opening doors or sitting down at restaurants since I was four years old.

I saw Uncle Saul's Porsche in the driveway. I hoped that we weren't delaying dinner. Generally, if I'm late, Mom goes ahead and serves. But as I was bringing Carl with me, I guess she was waiting.

"My Uncle Saul and Aunt Ceil are here tonight," I told Carl as I headed for the door.

"Wait up!" Carl called. "I gotta get all this stuff inside."

"Carl, Carl," I said. "This is Santa Amelia, not Manhattan. Your things are safe right where they are."

"I'm sorry," he said. "It may be safe as the church, but I've got a lot of years and police experience. Most things get stolen because their owners get careless. Humor me, Doris. I'll leave my suitcases in the trunk, but this . . . ." He indicated the gift-wrapped curtain rod. ". . . this has to go with me."

Evidently my folks had heard us pull up. The door opened before I could put a hand on the knob, and Mom swung the door wide in welcome. When I saw what she looked like, I could have died on the spot. But maybe I should explain about my mom.

Linda Fein is a joiner. Inevitably, the groups she belongs to are cultural and civil rights groups. In fact, Mom considers the Equal Rights Amendment a civil rights issue. You name the oppressed group, and she's done work for it. It goes back to when she was in college and was a heavily involved member of John Kennedy's New Frontier.

Hanging on the wall in her office, she has framed, signed letters of appreciation from *two* presidents: John F. Kennedy and Lyndon B. Johnson. Oh, yes, in the stronghold of Republican Southern California, Linda Fein is a *very* liberal Democrat. And tonight, it seemed, she had gone into liberal overkill. To make Carl feel "more welcome," she had dressed in a Saks Fifth Avenue version of a Japanese kimono-like dress, and had her hair up in an approximation of an Oriental style. I don't know how Carl felt about the apparition in the doorway, but I felt a deep, warm flush begin to spread up from my neck and across my face. I admit it, I blush easily.

"Welcome, welcome to our home," Mom said. I swear she almost bowed!

It must have been a funny picture we made. There was Carl in a three-piece Ivy League suit, with a long parcel over his shoulder. I was wearing a pair of jeans and a sweat shirt emblazoned with a picture of Felix Mendelssohn. And my mother was got up like a department store's idea of a geisha.

Carl was equal to the occasion. He really *did* bow. Face flaming, I followed them both into the house.

"May I take your parcel?" Mom asked, before I could even formally introduce Carl to her.

"I'll just put it here," Carl said, leaning it behind the door in the foyer. He then turned and extended his hand to my mom.

"You must be Doris's mother," he said with a big smile. "I'm Carl Suzuki."

"Call me Linda, Carl," Mom said. Then, turning with the air of a general who knows the troops will follow where she marches, led us both to the family room.

Uncle Saul and Dad were already shooting pool, with Aunt Ceil kibitzing from the sidelines. Aunt Ceil was dressed as though she were attending a soiree in Beverly Hills, and wore full evening makeup. I knew Mom must have told her to dress. Unnecessary, really. Ceil would dress to be in a mud-wrestling match. Color coordinated to match the mud, of course. As we came into the room, Dad was just making a difficult carom shot and Uncle Saul was looking on.

"Good shot!" Carl called appreciatively.

I took the initiative before Mom decided to do any

formal introductions. "This is my father, Carl," I said. "Doctor Michael Fein."

Without hesitation, Carl walked up and extended his hand to my Uncle Saul.

"Pleased to meet you, Doctor Fein," he said. Uncle Saul roared with laughter.

"Wrong Doctor Fein!" he laughed. "I'm Doctor Fein all right, but not the medical one. I'm the dental one, Doris's Uncle Saul. Pleased to meet you, Carl."

It was Carl's turn to blush. And he does, too. He gets a ruddy color when he's embarrassed. It was a natural mistake, I guess. When you consider my physical construction, I guess I *do* look more like Uncle Saul's daughter than my father's. Embarrassed or not, Carl carried it off.

"Well, I was half right, anyway," he grinned. "Nobody told me you were both doctors. I mean, Doris told me she had a dentist uncle. She says that's why her teeth are so pretty. Congratulations on your good work."

Uncle Saul beamed. "This is the other Doctor Fein," he said. "The one who only invites me to dinner so he can beat me at the pool table." Carl and Daddy shook hands. "But I beat him at the dinner table every time!" concluded Uncle Saul with a great chest-rumbling laugh.

He led Carl around the billiard table to where Aunt Ceil was seated.

"And this is my wife, Cecilia," he said.

"Call me Ceil," said my aunt. "And call me hungry, too. We've been waiting for dinner."

Tact isn't my Aunt Ceil's long suit. I guess from all

those years of being a featured skater, she became accustomed to star treatment. And Uncle Saul gives it to her, too. Frankly, I think she takes advantage of him. You may have heard the expression, Jewish-American princess? Well, my Aunt Ceil is too old to be a princess, but definitely acts like a dowager empress.

"Not our fault, Aunt Ceil," I said quickly, "Carl's plane was late."

"What's the rush?" my dad said. "We haven't even offered the man a drink before dinner! Besides, Ceil, you shouldn't be dwelling on the subject of dinner." Ceil colored. Since she stopped skating and getting all that exercise, she's constantly dieting. Before Ceil could get off a riposte, Daddy turned to Carl and said, "What'll it be?"

"Scotch with a tall soda, please," Carl said.

"You got it," Daddy said, walking over to the bar. "Chivas Regal okay?"

"Better than that." Carl smiled. "My brand!"

"Knew you had taste the minute I almost met you," Daddy quipped. "It's my brand, too."

"*I* knew he had taste when he came out to visit Doris," Mom said.

"Carl is here because his uncle is very ill," I said pointedly. I wasn't about to let Mom run off on my many virtues. She does that whenever I bring anyone male and eligible home.

"I would have come anyway," Carl said quickly. I gave him a sharp glance and immediately thought of the letter again. "Both our futures," it had said.

"Hope your uncle isn't seriously ill," Dad said.

"I'm afraid he is, Doctor Fein."

"Mike. Call me Mike."

"Okay . . . Mike," Carl said, smiling. "Well, I've been told by his doctor that my Uncle Jiichi has about six months to a year. I've never met him. It's too bad that I have to meet him this way, though."

"Never met your own uncle?" Ceil asked from across the room. "From what Doris has told us, Japanese are close knit, family-wise."

"My dad hates California," Carl explained. "He was living here in 1942, when the whole family was interned in Arizona. He went away and fought with the U.S. Army in Europe. When he got out, he swore he'd never come back here."

To her credit, Ceil shut up. I was getting distinctly uncomfortable with what I thought was going to be an enjoyable family dinner. Between my mom dressed up like a road company Madam Butterfly and my Aunt Ceil's notorious lack of tact, it promised to be quite an evening. I was mortified.

Mom broke the silence that hung over the room. "Well, I'm famished too," she said cheerily. "Let me see if Mary is ready to serve dinner."

I groaned inwardly. Mom had hired Mary, who cleans for us twice a week, to serve dinner. We don't have a maid, and we never have had one. I secretly hoped that Mom hadn't made Mary wear a uniform of some sort. She did that when I invited Harry Grubb to dinner once. Knowing that Harry is a millionaire, she rented a maid's outfit for Mary to serve dinner in.

It was quite uncomfortable at *La Maison Fein* that evening. I was dreading a repeat performance. Mom came back from the kitchen and took Carl's arm.

"Dinner is ready," she said. "Come with me, Carl.

Doris will be monopolizing you for most of your stay. I want you to sit with me. So we can get acquainted. I have so much to ask you about your culture."

I winced. Carl is a New York City-born-and-reared American of Japanese descent. As to being particularly mysterious and enigmatic, Carl is about as Oriental as McDonald's.

We sat down at the table and, before the first course was served, Mom said to Carl, "You know, Doris has told us about the wonderful meal she had at your Aunt Lucille's restaurant in New York. All that marvelous Japanese cooking. So, I've prepared a little surprise for you this evening. I worked most of the day on it. We'll be having a traditional Jewish dinner. Matzoh ball soup, boiled beef . . ."

I couldn't believe my eyes. Carl, who is an extremely polite man, suddenly burst out laughing. Mom broke off her recitation of the traditional menu and stared. Carl recovered his composure, but was still grinning widely as he said, "Forgive me, Linda. I wasn't laughing at you. It's just that I was born and raised in New York City. It struck me as hilarious that I've flown three thousand miles to a dinner of matzoh ball soup and *flanken!*"

"You know what *flanken* is?" queried Uncle Saul.

"I don't think there's a soul in New York City, Jew or Gentile, who doesn't!" Carl said with a smile. "I grew up eating Jewish cooking. In fact, my Aunt Lucille's silent partner in the restaurant was Mr. Berkowitz. They kept company for years and years. Aunt Lucille used to cook Jewish dishes for him. He didn't care for any Japanese dishes outside of the sashimi, the fish dishes."

Then seeing Mom's crestfallen look, he quickly

added, "But I love *flanken.* Tell me, do you make your own horseradish?"

"Uh, no," Mom admitted. "I drove all the way up to Farmer's Market in L.A. to get it fresh made, though."

"I'm sure I'll love it," Carl said.

We got through the dinner without any further incident or gaffes by my family. During the meal, Dad found out about Carl being a pool shooter, and immediately lined up a game. After the meal, which I only picked at, displaying great restrain, we all went back to the family room.

Dad is a pool shark. He claims that he used to make enough shooting pool while he was an intern to still court Mom in style. She was already a nurse when Dad was an intern, and making more money than he was. In a few seconds, we had chosen sides: Dad and me against Uncle Saul and Carl.

"Don't you want to use your own cue?" I asked Carl.

"I sure would, if it wasn't back in New York," said Carl, sighting down a cue he selected from the rack on the wall.

"But I thought from your letter that you were . . . I mean, if that isn't your cue in that package what is it?"

"What package?" Dad asked.

"It's behind the front door," Carl said. "And I told you what it was, Doris."

"You mean to tell me that you really do have a *sword* in there?" I asked.

"You bet," Carl said, stroking a shot at the triangle of racked balls. "It's very old, and it belongs to my Uncle Jiichi." With a sharp *crack* the pool balls scattered across the table. Two striped balls fell into pockets. Carl tried for a tough combination shot and missed. "Your shot, Doris," he said.

"I don't understand," Uncle Saul said, as I dropped the five ball into a side pocket. "I thought you said you'd never met your uncle."

"I haven't," Carl explained. "Uncle Jiichi used to be a kendo master, before the war. Kendo is the art of Japanese sword fighting. They don't use swords in training and matches, though. Too dangerous. They use split bamboo sticks that are the exact length and weight of swords. That, and masks and padding to protect themselves."

I missed my next shot and Dad took up his cue. He made three balls in rapid succession.

"But they do use swords at exhibitions," Carl continued. "The one in that package in the hall was made centuries ago, in Japan. My uncle hasn't seen it in thirty-seven years."

"How come?" I asked.

"Back in 1942," Carl explained, "when everyone was interned, such things were impounded by the government. My Uncle Jiichi saw which way the winds were blowing. He gave it to a Caucasian friend for safekeeping. Trouble is, while he was in the camp in Arizona, the people keeping it moved east to New York."

"How'd you get it back, then?" Dad asked.

"Well, my dad was in the U.S. Army," Carl said. "He was wounded in the Battle of the Bulge in Belgium. They sent him home. He went out west to visit the rest of the family at the camp . . ."

"That's outrageous!" cried my mother. "You mean to tell me that a wounded war hero had to visit his family

. . . an *American* family in a . . . concentration camp?"

"My dad always thought so," Carl admitted. "That's why he never came back to California. The memories were too strong. But he found out from my Uncle Jiichi where the sword was. Uncle got letters from the friends who had it. Pop promised Jiichi that, after the war, he'd put it in Uncle's hands. Personally. Uncle Jiichi was bitter. He told my father that the day would never come when the U.S. government would let any Japanese have a sword. Dad had more faith in our government."

"Misplaced faith, I'm afraid," Mom put in. "The President has signed a bill only this year to investigate the conditions in those camps, and to repay the loyal families that were imprisoned."

"How do you pay someone for four lost years, and the loss of everything he ever owned and worked to get?" Carl said with a trace of rancor. "It broke my Uncle Jiichi as a man. He had a truck farm, with a little nursery business on the side. He lost it all. When he got out of the camp, all he did was work as a gardener. He began to drink heavily too."

"Surely, he could have re-established himself somewhere, like your dad did," I said to Carl. "He opened that restaurant you told me about."

"Uncle Jiichi was old country-born," Carl said. "He was convinced that if he ever owned anything again, it would someday be taken away. Like I say, the internment broke him as a man. And I know of no way you can repay a man for loss of pride."

"You know I saw a show on T.V. about that," Aunt Ceil put in. "It must have been just awful for you, Carl."

"Not for me, it wasn't," Carl said with a smile. "I was born in New York five years after the war was over. The only hangover from those days was that Pop used to tell people he was Chinese. There was still a lot of hard feeling after the war ended, you know." Carl smiled ruefully. "He told people his name was Soo instead of Suzuki. But he never changed his name legally."

Dad quickly ran off the last of the balls remaining on the table. "Game ball," he said.

"We never stood a chance, Carl," Uncle Saul said. "He suckers everyone into a game of eight ball so he can win."

"But how come," Mom asked, not to be denied, "your uncle never got his sword back? After the war, I mean?"

"At first, he had no interest," Carl explained. "In anything. He got inside a bottle of booze and didn't come out until after I was born. By the time he was back on the rails, my folks couldn't afford the fare to California. They had a family to raise and were starting out their restaurant business."

"Why didn't you just ship it by mail?" I asked.

"That wasn't what my dad promised Uncle Jiichi in camp. He said he'd put the sword in Jiichi's hands *personally*. Now, Pop is too ill himself to be traveling around. He's retired and living in Florida. He has emphysema. But I'm his family delegate. I have to put the sword in Uncle Jiichi's hands before the old man dies."

"I think that's one of the saddest stories I've ever heard," said Mom. I looked over at her. She was actually close to tears. In that instant, I forgave her the entire grotesque evening and all the uncomfortable moments.

Say what you will about my mom, she believes whole-heartedly in all the things she does to help others. Her overboard attitude may embarrass me sometimes, but when Linda Fein believes in something, get out of the way. Or you might have a Linda Fein-sized hole in you.

"Oh, don't feel so bad, Linda," Carl said easily. "What's done is done. Most of the folks it actually happened to don't even discuss it. They figure it's over. Let's think about the future. It's only in the past few years that it's all come out in the papers. And that's because the Japanese Americans *my* age are bringing it to the public eye. They're rightfully indignant. They feel their parents got the shaft, and want amends made."

Carl glanced at his watch. I got the hint. The discussion was getting rather heavy, and he was uncomfortable.

"I think Carl has to be going soon, Mother," I said.

"Oh, must you?" Mom asked. "We've hardly begun to know each other."

"Plenty of time for that, Linda," Dad said. "Carl's got two weeks, don't you, Carl?"

"Sure do," Carl said. "Don't worry, Linda. You'll see more than enough of me. Tomorrow, Doris has promised to take me out to see the gray whales migrate, offshore."

"Wonderful!" Mom said. "You know that I joined Greenpeace the same time as Doris did?"

"You've joined everything from Save the Whales to Hadassah," Uncle Saul quipped. "You have enough cards in your wallet to play bridge with!"

"Never you mind, Saul Fein," Mom said indignantly.

"If *some* of us didn't act, the world would be a sorry place!"

"Hear, hear," said Carl. "I think you're a wonderful, dedicated lady, Linda. And I appreciate what you said. There should be more folks like you."

"Thank you, kind sir," said Mom, giving Uncle Saul a look. "Nice to be appreciated by *someone.*" She looked around the room challengingly, as if waiting for anyone to say another word. No one did. We all knew better.

I didn't say anything because my mind was elsewhere. I was still thinking about driving Carl to his hotel in Los Angeles. I was sure he wanted to talk about what he'd said in the letter. And I still hadn't figured out what I was going to say to him. "Listen Carl," I said, "it's really a bit late for me to drive you to L.A. and then drive back again tomorrow to pick you up. How about I loan you my car?"

"Doris!" my mother said in shock. "He doesn't know how to get there."

"Nothing to it," Uncle Saul said. "You just take Main Street to the San Diego Freeway northbound, get off at . . ."

In a few minutes, we were all involved in the Southern California pastime of giving directions and offering favorite routes to somewhere. Every SoCal resident has two bibles: one for his faith and the other a Thomas Brothers highway-and-street directory map.

I walked with Carl to the car and handed him the keys. My family stood in the driveway and doorway to wave good-bye.

"I wanted to talk to you alone, Doris," Carl said softly,

as he got behind the wheel of the Gumdrop.

"Plenty of time tomorrow, after you've seen your Uncle Jiichi," I said elusively. "Sure you can find your way back?"

"Absolutely." Carl smiled. He held up my Thomas Brothers map. "With this in my hand, and love in my heart, you couldn't keep me away."

Not caring that my folks were looking, I bent over and kissed him quickly on the lips. Then I waved as he started up the Gumdrop and pulled away from the curb. When I got back to where my family was gathered, waving, my Aunt Ceil, with typical finesse, said, "You know? I was watching the way that man looks at you, Doris. I think he's serious about you."

"What if he is, Ceil?" Uncle Saul said, putting an arm around her. "He seems like a nice young man."

"He's hardly Jewish," Ceil said elaborately.

"So what?" Dad said, with a wink at me. "He's got half the requirements: he's a professional man . . . a lawyer!"

3/The Parvenu Afloat

"I don't see why we have to wait in the parking area," grumbled Harry Grubb. "I left word at the gate, with the attendant. We could be waiting in someplace civilized. Like the bar."

"It won't be long," I said. "Carl is very punctual. He should be here . . ." I glanced at my watch and then, as I looked up, saw Carl enter the parking lot of The Cortez Yacht Club in the Gumdrop. ". . . right now!" I concluded in triumph.

Carl spotted us and waved. He still had the top down on the Gumdrop. Maybe he couldn't get it back on unassisted. He pulled up at the parking attendant's desk, handed the keys to a uniformed man, and came over to us.

"Carl! Great to see you again!" said Harry Grubb, pumping Carl's hand.

"His joy is directly attributable to being able to go to the bar now," I said.

"Nonsense, Doris," Harry drawled in his nasal Midwestern twang. "My joy is that now we can go to the bar *on my boat.*"

We followed as Harry led the way down the boarded walk that ran alongside the yacht slips. I noted Carl's expression as we walked past each rank of yachts. The Cortez has a system for the way they tie up yachts. The sail-powered yachts get the slips visible through the picture windows of the clubhouse. The power yachts are further down. Harry maintains it's snobbism.

Harry has always complained about the long walk to his end of the boardwalk. He once threatened to buy an electric golf cart so he could ride from the clubhouse to his boat. The yacht club reciprocated by telling him that he'd be bounced out if he did.

Eventually, Harry gave in. Rich as he is, he couldn't buy the Cortez, the way he did *The Santa Amelia Register.* There are members there who are richer than Harry, if you can imagine that.

We walked past the sailing craft, each one getting bigger and more elaborate. We finally got to the power yacht section, where we had to begin again, with yachts of medium to progressively larger sizes.

"There ought to be a way station, or an oasis, along here," Harry muttered. "I joined this phony club to go boating, not hiking."

"You never get any exercise except jumping to conclusions," I said. "The walk will do you good. Besides, we're here."

Carl looked at the craft tied up at the pier and gave a long, toneless whistle. I'm used to Harry's yacht, so it didn't occur to me that Carl wasn't prepared for the sight. The Parvenu is about a hundred feet long, and powered by monstrous diesel engines. It was built in the 1930s and is opulent enough for a Greek shipping magnate: Croesus. Harry noted Carl's outright amazement at the sight of the Parvenu and cracked, "They threw in two pairs of oars when I bought it. I just couldn't resist such a bargain."

"Did you get the galley slaves that go with the oars?" Carl asked.

"Set them free immediately," Harry replied, utterly deadpan. "Today, they own a car wash in San Diego. Doing better than I am, too."

"Sure, sure," said Carl. "We'll get up a benefit for you, Harry."

Harry grinned. That's his kind of conversation. Despite his almost-eighty years, Harry often acts like a kid with a new toy when it comes to his money. I guess it comes from being poor most of his life.

"I always wanted a yacht," he explained as we went up the gangway, where a uniformed crewman waited at the rail. "This one was going for back taxes that some movie producer couldn't pay . . ."

"Good afternoon, Mr. Grubb," said the crewman.

"It certainly is, Ismael," Harry replied. As we strolled toward the midships, where the saloon was located, Harry said over his shoulder, "That man is a dreadful sailor and a worse cook. But when I found out his name, I had to hire him. I've never gotten over reading *Moby Dick*. True, he's an Ismael, not an Ishmael. But it's the Spanish equivalent."

"Does that make you Ahab?" Carl quipped.

"Hell, no!" Harry snorted. "I'm no captain. I couldn't tell a binnacle from a barnacle. In fact, here comes the captain now."

"Afternoon, Harry," said the short, stocky man in

white who approached us. "Ready to go when you are."

"Do you mind not using that expression, 'ready to go when you are?' " Harry said. "At my age, it has other connotations. Couldn't you say something more nautical, you old pirate?"

"How about ready to shove off?" asked the captain.

Harry groaned in response. "That's no better," he said. "How about 'set sail?' "

The captain waved his arm about him. "If you find any sails aboard, I'll set them. Hell, Harry. I'd eat them!"

"Better eating than Ismael's cooking. I think his last name is Borgia!"

"If you don't stop complaining," the captain said, smiling, "I'll refuse to drink any more of your scotch, and I won't let you win at gin rummy!"

"This pirate's name is Jack Ford," said Harry to us. "He masquerades as a captain. Actually, he's a card shark with a master's ticket. Jack, this is Carl Suzuki, a friend of mine from New York. You already know Doris Fein."

"Sure do. Hi there, Miss Fein. And nice meeting you, Mr. Suzuki."

"I'm Carl," said Carl, shaking hands. "Mr. Suzuki is my father."

I didn't comment on Jack calling me "Miss" Fein. It's a lost cause. He's an old school yacht captain, and to him the word "Ms." doesn't exist. If he doesn't know your marital status or preference of address, he persists in calling you Miss. If he met the Queen Mother and didn't know her, he'd call her Miss.

"You can take her out when you're ready, Jack,"

Harry said. "You all set on where we're going?"

"Just go into the saloon and sit down," said Captain Jack. "Stop trying to impress people with that owner stuff. We should spot the whales just outside the harbor. Then on to Santa Catarina for dinner. They expect us, and your reservations at the Camelot Hotel are confirmed."

"What's all this?" Carl asked. "I thought we were only going out a little way to see the whales, then come back here."

Harry waved a long, thin hand. "It costs almost as much to crank up this white elephant for a cruise to Santa Catarina as it does to go offshore a few miles. Much as I trust Blackbeard here, I don't like cruising at night. Thought we'd overnight it on the island. On me."

The island Harry was referring to is Santa Catarina, just twenty miles offshore. Like its big sister island, Catalina, it boasts an elaborate casino, ballroom, hotel, and a rather small resort town surrounding its protected harbor. There are people who live on the island year round, but mostly it's the tourist trade that makes the island solvent.

In its heyday, the island and its casino were powerful attractions to the very rich and newly rich from the Hollywood film colony. Unlike Catalina, there was never a ferry service to Santa Catarina Island in the 1920s and 1930s. You just didn't go there unless you had a yacht. Or a friend who had one. After World War Two, when millionaires began keeping a lower profile, a ferry service was instituted. The old-timers on the island still grouse about the influx of tourists with funny hats and cheap cameras that invade them each year from April to October.

A deep bass rumble set off slight vibrations in the saloon of the yacht where we sat. Carl gave a little start at the first tremors.

"Starting up," Harry declared. "Beautiful weather for it. You enjoy sailing, Carl?"

"I couldn't say," Carl replied. "Up until now, the most sailing I ever did was in a rowboat on Central Park Lake."

"Don't worry about a thing, my boy," Harry said cheerily. "Captain Jack and I have made this trip scores of times, and he hasn't hit an iceberg yet." Seeing Carl's sudden look of apprehension, Harry added, "Just kidding, Carl. You'll love it!"

He didn't. As soon as we left the calm waters of the harbor and got into the offshore ground swells, Carl made a beeline for the rail. He was either sick or in between whoopses for the entire trip.

The whales appeared as promised, and it was a thrilling sight. The gray whales breed in the warm, protected waters of the Sea of Cortez in Baja California. Which is really part of Mexico, not California. Each year, they migrate from the cold waters off Alaska down to Baja for mating season.

Even when you watch them through a telescope from the shore, you get no idea of the incredible majesty of these creatures. One whale, seen close up, is stunning. An entire group of them, or a pod, as they call it, is almost beyond comprehension. I spotted a straggler close by the rail where Carl stood, looking green.

"Look, Carl, a whale!" I cried, pointing at the leviathan.

"Tell me when you see a tree," said Carl smiling sickly. "That's all I want to see right now. A nice tree, rooted in good, solid ground." He suddenly felt another spasm, and took off for the other side of the yacht. I guess he didn't want me to see him be sick. Silly "manly" pride.

By the time we entered the harbor at Camelot, the one town on the island, he was feeling a lot better. He came to the rail as I pointed out landmarks of the town that sparkled in the brilliant April sunshine.

The town is shaped like a bent horseshoe, conforming to the line of its harbor. At the cusp of the crescent stands the Camelot Casino. Built sixty years ago, it stands as solid and graceful as the rugged hills that descend to the sea behind it. The structure is set on huge concrete piers at the far end, and a boardwalk above the water encircles the rounded, high cupola'd building.

Behind the Casino and to its right is another building, matching the architectural style, which is best described as Mediterranean Art Deco. That's the Camelot Hotel. Smaller structures eventually give way to cottages and bungalows. Further back in the hills there are some mansions, but they aren't visible from the harbor. Beyond them lie the rocky, sparsely vegetated hills. Where the buffalo roam. That's right, buffalo. They have them running wild on the island. I don't know how they got there, so don't ask. There are wild goats too.

I have a friend, Vick Knight, who is an expert on the island. He says that there's a species of lizard that lives on the island and is found nowhere else in the world. He tells me that, like the Galápagos Islands that so fascinated Darwin, the California channel islands are biologically unique.

I couldn't care less about lizards. Not that they frighten me, or any of that nonsense. I just never have been able to work up much enthusiasm over reptiles. But, as I say, Santa Catarina is a lovely and fascinating place.

"All ashore that's going ashore!" called Harry Grubb from the doorway to the saloon, where he'd spent the trip playing gin rummy with Captain Jack.

Jack only takes the helm when we go in and out of the harbors. Once he sets the course, he goes down to the saloon, and he and Harry play gin. I don't know why Harry bothers to own the Parvenu. It would be a lot cheaper to sell the boat and hire Captain Jack as a card partner. Harry never sees the ocean or stands on deck to get the spray and the salt air. He could just as easily be in his mansion in Santa Amelia Estates.

"I was ready to go ashore five minutes after we left," Carl called. "Don't get between me and dry land."

"You two go ahead and see the town," Harry called. "I want to finish the game with Jack. Once he gets this battleship tied up. I've got him on a blitz so far. He'll be working for free for the next month!"

"Aren't you coming ashore at all?" I asked.

"Of course, of course," Harry answered impatiently. "I'll see you at the hotel. The reservations are in my name. This is important, what I'm doing here! It's ... principle, that's what it is. First time I've been ahead of the old pirate since we started playing eight years ago."

I glanced at Carl and shrugged. He grinned and we

set off to see the sights of Santa Catarina or, properly, the town of Camelot.

The town itself isn't large at all. It consists of a half mile of waterfront lined with one-story shop buildings, each with a false second floor to make it look taller. The false facades are elaborately decorated with the building trim popular in the 1920s: gazelles and goddesses, vines and baskets of fruit, all painted in bright colors.

Most of the shop fronts were undergoing painting. The new annual onslaught of tourists would begin in earnest over the Memorial Day weekend, five weeks hence. The shopkeepers would be ready with what Harry Grubb calls the island's "desert-charm-of-the-sand-and-the-palms." To Harry, that translates as the sand on the beach, and the palms that are outstretched for money.

I hadn't been to Santa Catarina in a few years. In a way, it was a down trip. The quality of the merchandise available at the stores downtown had taken a sharp nose dive. There were all sorts of flimsy gimcracks with decals that proclaimed them souvenirs of the island. From the badly applied decals, I felt sure that half the merchandise was imported from Hong Kong or Taiwan.

But Carl, having no standard of comparison, was greatly taken by the town. Most of all, by the fact that there are three motor vehicles on the entire island: a police car, a fire engine, and an ambulance. The rest of the residents get around on bicycles, golf carts, and in the case of the hill residents, on horseback. Being a New Yorker, and accustomed to breathing a mixture of soot and car fumes, Carl found it strangely non-toxic.

We were slowly making our way toward the Camelot

Hotel when I saw someone familiar go by in an electric golf cart. She was moving at a brisk five miles per hour, steering the cart around the bicyclists, so I got a good look at her. It didn't register with me at first who she was; I hadn't seen her since I was thirteen. Five years ago. I grabbed at Carl's arm and said, "I know that lady!"

"Mrs. Grayson!" I called. "Helen Grayson!"

She stopped the golf cart and looked around her.

"Over here!" I cried, waving my hand.

She put the cart into reverse and backtracked to where Carl and I stood in front of a T-Shirt store. She stopped directly alongside us and looked straight at me, unrecognizingly. Then a smile lit up her face.

"Why, Doris Fein, of all people!" she said. "You look simply marvelous. I didn't know you at first. My dear, you've lost so much weight."

"Carl," I said, changing the subject quickly. "This is Mrs. Helen Grayson. She was my piano teacher when I was a little girl. Mrs. Grayson, this is my friend, Carl Suzuki. He's visiting from New York City."

"Delighted, Carl," she said, smiling broadly. "Doris is very kind. She didn't mention that I was also her mother's piano teacher. Back before the Crimean War."

"Impossible," Carl said, shaking her hand. "You can't be a day over eighteen yourself!"

"How would you like to take a ride in my cart, young man?" she said, with an impish grin. "Talk like that, and I'll take you anywhere."

In truth, Mrs. Grayson does wear well. She has to be over sixty at this point, but she looks for all the world like a woman in her early fifties. Her figure is trim for her age, her eyes are clear, her skin tone fresh and rosy. She has wrinkles, of course, but what woman her age wouldn't? She's the kind of old lady I'd like to be when I start getting on. She isn't trying to hide her age with makeup or hair dyes. She is simply a beautiful woman who wears her age with dignity and a soap-washed charm. But when she got out of her golf cart, I was shocked.

She reached alongside her, and grabbed one of those tripod-footed walking sticks you see handicapped people use sometimes. Carl immediately offered a hand to help her out. Mrs. Grayson caught my look of shock.

"You didn't know, did you, Doris?" she said gently, in a well-modulated voice. "I had a stroke five years ago. Not long after I despaired of teaching you those Bach preludes and fugues. I retired to the island about then."

"I . . . didn't know," I said. Inside, my heart ached. Mrs. Grayson had always been so *active.* All I had known about her was that she gave piano lessons to the middle-class families of Santa Amelia and gave away lessons to any promising, less fortunate kid. Each year, her students would give a recital at the Santa Amelia High auditorium. I was never good enough for those programs.

Now, to see such a vital person walking with a stick and dragging her left leg saddened me more than I could convey to her in words.

For the next five minutes or so, Carl stood by in considerate silence as Mrs. Grayson asked about my family, some other folks in Santa Amelia, and generally, how things were going for me. I had just about brought her up to date when I saw Harry Grubb's long, lean form come striding down Main Street.

There's no mistaking Harry Grubb. He's six-feet-four-inches tall, thin and erect as a flagpole, with a mane of white hair and matching full beard. Carl waved to him, and he came over and joined us.

When I introduced them to each other, I was stunned at Harry's reaction. Ordinarily, Harry respects no person, no institution, no matter how sacred. Harry would make jokes at his own funeral. But after the how-dyoudos, Harry gave a courtly sort of half-bow and said, "Mrs. Grayson, had I known someone as lovely as yourself resided upon this clinker in the channel, I would have swum it, as Leander swam the Hellespont, just for the sight and sound of you!"

Now that is the single, fruitiest speech I have ever heard in my life. If anyone had said it to me, I would have laughed. But not Mrs. Grayson. I guess there really is a generation gap after all. You'd have thought that Harry had given her an armful of roses.

"You are kind, sir," she said, smiling. "But your charm would be more appreciated were you to arrive dry and rested. I'm glad you have come by boat."

" 'Was this the face that launched a thousand ships, And burnt the topless towers of Ilium?' " quoted Harry.

"This Helen has trouble with her own mortality, Mr. Grubb," Mrs. Grayson said with a dazzling smile. "I hope you didn't expect what the rest of the passage demands?"

"What the hell are they talking about?" whispered Carl.

"It's a quote from Marlowe's *Dr. Faustus,*" I said

softly. "The next line goes, 'Sweet Helen, make me immortal with a kiss.' "

"Why the romantic old billy goat!" Carl said, chuckling.

Harry was still plying Helen Grayson with his septuagenarian charms.

"We are off to the hotel to have a cleanup and dinner," he was saying. "I'd be honored if you would join us."

"The dinner sounds fine," she said. "I have some errands to run and grocery shopping to do, though. If you like, I can give you a lift to the far end of the street. That way, we can leave these young people to themselves, and you can tell me where you learned your Christopher Marlowe."

"Done!" said Harry.

"And done!" I echoed. "Carl has never seen Camelot. We'd prefer to walk, wouldn't we, Carl?"

"Sure," said Carl with a wink at Harry. "See you at the hotel, you poetic devil!"

We watched the two of them ride off in the golf cart. Once they were a block away, I saw Harry Grubb uncoil one long arm and drape it across the back of the cart's seat, behind Helen Grayson's shoulders.

"Did you see that?" I asked Carl.

"It's spring, Doris," he said. "And, in spring, you're as old as you feel."

"Really?" I inquired. "And how old do you feel?"

"Ask me after I've had some solid food." He smiled. "I emptied out on the way over here."

4/A Dreadful Dinner and a Crashing Ball

I remembered the Camelot Hotel as something special, but I hadn't seen it in years. When I was twelve years old, I had come to the island with my parents for a weekend stay. For me, it had been a castle in some super fairyland.

Most of all, I had remembered the lobby, a huge, wide-spaced affair with an open cocktail lounge in one corner. There had been a Maxfield Parrish painting about six-by-three feet on the wall facing the registration desk. Etched, blue-mirrored panels, illuminated from above and below, revealed rows of top-hatted Fred Astaire lookalikes merrily clinking champagne glasses with rows of almost-Ginger Rogerses, their ranks disappearing finally into a mirrored infinity. Only the bubbles that rose from their glasses remained in the foreground—bits of merriment, frozen in space and time.

The deep maroon plush rug had felt more like a lawn than a carpet underfoot. Massive lounge chairs dotted the lobby, where gleaming arches of chrome enclosed luxurious puffs of maroon velvet. In the center of the lobby was the focus of attention: an illuminated statuary fountain in the shape of the goddess, Diana, running with a brace of greyhounds. The goddess in the fountain, however, wore a 1930s hairdo and strongly resembled the almost-Gingers on the mirrored panels in the lounge.

In the six years since I'd seen it, nothing had changed. Perhaps I should say, nothing *had been* changed. It was still the same carpet, but with six years of tourist footprints written on its now patched and trampled pile. The newer sections of the carpet were a discernibly different shade of maroon, and definitely cheaper looking in quality. The fountain goddess was gone, leaving a forlorn, dry circle of white-painted concrete in the center of the lobby. The Parrish painting was gone and unreplaced.

Some sections of the mirrored blue panels were cracked. One entire panel of blue mirror had been replaced by an unetched, untinted one, leaving an almost-Astaire raising his glass to the reflection of a door marked FIRE EXIT. I could have cried.

But through the haze of neglect and grime, the stylistic intent of the lobby still shone. Like a once-beautiful woman, abused by years and ill-used by strangers, it still retained a certain frayed-hem charm.

"Interesting décor," Carl said.

"You should have seen it years ago," I found myself saying for the fourth or fifth time that day. It seemed that everywhere we had walked on our way to the hotel, the entire town was somehow a bit out at the elbow. Unaccountably, I kept justifying the overall aura of seediness to Carl. Perhaps I wanted to retain my dream of Camelot and deny its rundown reality. I forget who said that dreams die hard, but it sure is true.

"Do you want to sign in at the desk?" Carl asked.

"Not right now, Carl. First, I have to call my folks again."

I'd tried reaching them on Harry's radio phone on the yacht, but got only the answering machine. I hate those things. Being a Saturday, I knew Dad had already closed up the office and would be at the Santa Amelia Raquetball Club. Lord only knows what organization meeting Mom was attending and where. I didn't want her to be concerned about my whereabouts.

Not that I had to tell her, mind you. I am my own person, eighteen years of age, and a registered voter. It's a matter of consideration for my folks' feelings, and they *would* worry about me. Nor was my spending the night away cause for concern. I've done that before, too.

I'd even thought it rather silly that Harry Grubb had secured rooms for us at the Camelot Hotel. There was more than enough room to sleep on the Parvenu. But Harry is an Edwardian, if not a Victorian. Despite his being on board as "chaperone" for Carl and me, something I found rather quaint, he felt it would be more "proper" if Carl and I had separate rooms at the hotel. Either that, or he intended to be up drinking and playing gin rummy noisily with Captain Jack most of the night and didn't want to be disturbed.

I went to an old-fashioned phone booth in the corner

of the sad lobby and dialed the mainland. Got the darned machine again. As soon as I got the pre-recorded message in my mother's voice and heard the *beeep*, I spoke hurriedly into the recorder.

"It's-me-Mom-I'm-on-Santa-Catarina-at-the-hotel-be -back-tomorrow-early-please-don't-worry-no-emer-gency-just-too-late-to-sail-back-tonight-love-you-both." Then I rejoined Carl, and we went into the dining room, where Harry Grubb and Mrs. Grayson were already seated with cocktails set up in front of them.

The dining room was the same threadbare version of elegance that had saddened me in the lobby. No point in going into it, really. As we approached the table, Harry, ever the old-school gentleman, stood up.

"Ah, the younger set," he drawled, smiling to reveal his large, tobacco-stained teeth. "Have you come to dinner, or only to remind me of my impending mortality? For a few moments, we were both reliving palmier days."

"Mr. Grubb is a vanishing breed," smiled Helen Grayson. "A real romantic. Do sit down, children. He's a marvelous talker."

In the past, I have found Harry Grubb to be as romantic as a food fight in a high school cafeteria. He utterly despises sentimentality of any sort, and consistently sneers at others who display it. This newly displayed facet of Harry's character fascinated me. I also decided to have some fun at his expense. As soon as we sat down, I said, "Oh yes, I know. He's constantly quoting Byron, Keats, and Shelley in the office of the *Santa Amelia Register*. The entire staff knows and loves his poetic nature."

In point of fact, Harry is renowned at *The Register* for his vitriolic sense of humor and a vocabulary so explicit that the air around his desk often turns blue. With small electric sparks visible. Surprisingly, I got a no-no look from Harry, indicating that I shouldn't pursue this conversational tack.

I gave Harry a look as if to say, I understand. You want to make a nice impression on this lady. Harry almost gave an audible sigh of relief. Carl and I sat down and a middle-aged waitress, in a uniform that must have fit her once, appeared and put the menus on the table.

"Thought we'd wait to order until you got here," Harry explained.

For the next few minutes, we studied the menu. It was one of those cutesie-poo affairs that has the entrées describing themselves in first person. I selected a dish called lobster à la Camelot, which described itself as: "I'm the mariner's delight. A whole California lobster, split and broiled, stuffed with juicy shrimp and luscious crabmeat. Served with oceans of drawn butter, French fries, and your choice of salad or our own special New England-style clam chowder." Carl ordered the same, Mrs. Grayson, a seafood salad and Harry, his inevitable New York cut sirloin with the usual accoutrements. He also ordered a bottle of California chablis for us and a glass of red wine for himself.

I should have been warned by the deteriorating décor, and have assumed that the quality of the food had declined apace. The dinner was simply dreadful. No other words could describe the microwave-thawed, portion-controlled mess that arrived lukewarm twenty minutes later. The meals, all of them, were stultifyingly bad.

I saw Carl take one mouthful of the stuffed lobster, and the expression on his face was one of mingled shock and utter disbelief. I couldn't help it. I burst out laughing. Harry, worrying at his steak without any discernible effect, remarked:

"I don't know whether to call for another steak knife or a chisel!" He put his knife to one side. "I don't know about you folks, but this is totally inedible."

"Some of this may have once been vegetable," observed Mrs. Grayson over her salad, "but I doubt it."

"I'm writing to the *Guide Michelin* when I get back to the mainland," Harry said. "I feel this restaurant rates three stomach pumps and a black flag."

"With a skull and crossbones on it," Carl added.

The dreadful dinner then became a gag (pun intended), each of us trying to outdo each other in decrying its awfulness. As you might expect, Harry Grubb won.

"I may send Ismael over here to give their chef lessons," Harry snorted.

"And I must send myself home," Helen Grayson added. She began to stand. Harry immediately got to his feet and helped her from the table.

"I'll see you home, Helen," he said.

"No, no, Harry," she protested. "I have my cart outside. I'll just buzz on home." With an impish look, she added, "I don't want to spoil anyone's dinner."

"I won't hear of it," Harry said. "You could suddenly get a gastric seizure on the way home. I should go with you for your own safety."

"If you'd really been concerned for all our safety, you'd never have invited us to dinner here," I said. Harry shrugged eloquently.

"I haven't been here in five years," he said. "I eat on board. I asked Captain Jack what was the best restaurant on the island. I should have realized that any man who plays cards the way he does could hardly be a gourmet."

"It's not your fault, Harry," Helen Grayson said soothingly. "It *was* quite fine at one time. It's just that, lately, everything seems to have gone downhill on Santa Catarina. Either that, or what's in memory is always better than present reality."

"No, the food *had* to be better back then," Harry Grubb decided aloud. "Otherwise no one would have survived to remember it." He took Mrs. Grayson's arm.

"Please, Harry. Don't disrupt your evening. I'll be fine getting home," she said.

"But I won't be, without your company. I insist on accompanying you."

"Oh dear," she said. "I live at the far end of town and up a very steep hill. That's why I have the cart. How would you get back here, or to your yacht?"

"No problem. I can walk."

"At your age?" I asked, rather untactfully, and got a baleful look from Harry in return.

"I will have you know that my doctor says I am in superb condition for a man of my years," he said huffily.

"And I want you to stay that way," said Helen, easily.

"I know," Carl volunteered. "Go together. Harry can take the cart back to the Parvenu and recharge it at the dock. It does take a 220 volt plug, doesn't it?"

"Errr, yes," Helen replied. "I have a transformer that I plug it into at night."

"There you are!" Carl said. "I saw a 220 outlet on the dock."

"He's right, Helen," said Harry, smiling hugely. "I'll have your cart in front of your door at six tomorrow morning. Then we can have a decent breakfast on the Parvenu. Ismael may have Borgia bloodlines, but even *he* can't screw up scrambled eggs and bacon."

Helen Grayson gave Harry a lovely smile and said, "If you are so gallant as to see me home and still be up that early, I'll make you a real breakfast. Steak and eggs, hotcakes, juice, plenty of fresh ground coffee, and biscuits. A real *man*'s breakfast."

Harry looked like a small boy who had just received a set of electric trains for Christmas. His face lit up brighter than any tree, and he said with obvious feeling, "Helen, I haven't had a meal like that for breakfast since I left Chicago. People in California seem to eat only to survive. That's a real farmer's breakfast . . . a feast! My man, Bruno, prepares what my doctor suggests, and only that. He's devoted but, as a cook, uninspired at breakfast."

"I wouldn't want you to break your diet, Harry."

"Beautiful lady, I lived for more than seventy years on meals like you describe for breakfast. I am still here. And hungry already. I think even my doctor would approve this once."

"Then I really must go," Helen Grayson said. "I'll have to take a steak out of the freezer to thaw."

"Not at all," Harry said, smiling. "I'll have Ismael get a couple of filets from my refrigerator on the Parvenu.

I shudder to think of what he'd do to them, anyway. . . . What is that?" Harry cocked an ear, like a robin listening for a worm. We all fell silent for a moment.

"That's from the Casino Ballroom," Helen said after listening for a second. "They're playing *Moonlight Serenade*, Glenn Miller's old theme song."

"You mean the Miller Band is at the Casino?" Harry said happily. "Why don't we all go? It's not that late!"

A cloud passed over Helen Grayson's face. "I . . . don't go there at all," she said. "It's all dance music, and . . ." she glanced down eloquently at the tripod walking stick at her side.

"Forgive me," Harry said hurriedly. "It was unthinking of me. I just wanted somehow to prolong the time with you. . . . I . . ." He suddenly became aware of Carl and me and turned bright red. ". . . I'll see you home."

"Do you want to go to the Casino Ballroom, Carl?" I asked.

"You know how I love big bands," he smiled. "Besides, I don't think I'd care to stay here for dessert!"

We all laughed, and Harry went off with Helen, promising that he'd see us in the morning. On the short walk from the hotel to the Casino, I was relieved to find that Carl had tabled his "important" talk for a while. He hadn't pressed the issue during our stroll alone that afternoon, either.

If the hotel had been ill-maintained, the Casino certainly hadn't. The fifty-year-old building looked as new and shiny as the day it had opened its doors in the unpromising year of 1930. The wood and glass sparkled, the boardwalk was impeccably kept with a number of new planks that I could see in the light of the bright lamps that lined the circular, elevated walkway.

The lobby was magnificent with its high ceiling and its walls lined with artwork of the Deco period. There was one entire wall devoted to old photographs of the elegant dance palace. There were shots of the dance floor filled with couples in white dinner jackets and evening gowns, looking once more up to date, and in fashion. The old 1930's elegance is coming back for evening wear. I find it hard to reconcile with everyone dressing like a cowboy in the daytime, though.

There was also a big section of formal shots of the great bands that had played at the Casino Ballroom over the years. Carl was fascinated. He pointed out one after another, each new discovery delighting him.

"Look at this shot! That's the Glen Gray Orchestra . . . The Casa Loma, they called it . . . and Phil Harris . . . Charlie Barnet, Jack Jameson, Artie Shaw. . . . Oh, Doris, this is just great!"

I don't know too much about the big bands. Sure, I know some of the more famous ones. We have a radio station somewhere up in the San Gabriel Valley that plays nothing but big band music. I listen to it sometimes on the radio in the Gumdrop. But Carl is a genuine big band freak, though all sorts of music appeal to him. When it comes to those old orchestras, he's just as rabid in his own field as Larry Small is about rock 'n' roll.

I sighed with inner relief, thinking about Larry Small. Since he finally got the job he wanted on *Rolling Stone Magazine*, he was now safely four-hundred miles away in San Francisco. He had certainly cramped my style in New York. I was happy to know that he'd have no chance to do it again.

"Harry James!" Carl was saying. "I'm not sure who

that girl vocalist is, though. I don't think Jo Stafford was with him back then . . ."

"*Mister* Suzuki," I said. "Are you going to stand in the lobby all night, dwelling in the past? Or aren't you interested in going inside?"

Carl snapped out of his reverie like a swimmer surfacing. He took a deep breath. "Sorry, Doris. It's just that we don't have many places like this in New York. We don't seem to cherish our past. Just tear it all down to make way for the future. But this one here, this picture ought to interest you. It's an all-woman big band, Ina Ray Hutton's. They were a hard swinging group, too. Not like Phil Spitalny and his All-girl Orchestra."

"All-*woman*, don't you mean?"

"Oh, stop accusing me of indirect chauvinism, Doris. That's the official title of the band. They were advertised that way. And here's still another group. See? They called themselves the same thing: Evylyn Phillips and her All-girl Band. I glanced at the old photo and saw a sixteen-woman band, all wearing identical white evening gowns, all blonds, and all permed. Except for the lady who had to be Evylyn. She alone was wearing a dark gown and had dark hair. You couldn't tell from the photo if her dress and hair were black or red. The old-time film didn't show a difference between red and black. That's why in old movies on TV, the women look like they're wearing black lipstick.

"Very interesting," I said. "But I'd like to go inside and maybe dance a bit."

"Gee, I'm sorry, Doris. Sometimes I get carried away," he said, grinning. "At least it's an inexpensive hobby. I could be crazy about old cars."

"Deliver me!" I cried. "My Uncle Saul is a stone-car freak. You just saw his Porsche the other night. He has an old Packard and a reproduction of a 1932 Auburn Boat-tailed Speedster. He and Harry get together, and I'm bored stiff."

"You don't like old cars?"

"I love them. I like to ride in them. I enjoy driving them. But my idea of a good time is not discussing vacuum spark advances, roller-bearing front ends and manifold cutouts. Whatever *they* are."

Actually, that's not true. I know very well what makes an automobile stop and go. When I got the Gumdrop, I made up my mind that I'd never be one of those fluttering, helpless types standing on a freeway alongside a car that wouldn't go. And have no idea what was wrong. I know the owner's maintenance manual on the TR-7 from cover to cover. I just don't feel I want to make an evening's entertainment out of it.

"Well then, shall we join the dancing feet?" Carl asked, offering his arm. Humming the theme from the film *42nd Street,* we purchased tickets and entered the Ballroom.

It's magnificent. When you enter, the bandstand is at the far side of the room, flanked by huge curved windows that look out on the sea, framing the stage. The dance floor is tremendous, capable of accomodating five hundred couples. Behind a brass-and-wood railing that circumscribes the circular dance floor are tables and chairs that can seat that many and more. The décor is Art Deco as at the Camelot Hotel, but this was so lovingly maintained that I felt I had stepped backwards in time to the 1930s.

They also have the largest reflector ball in the country hanging above the dance floor. If you've never seen one in a disco or in a movie, it's a huge globe, suspended from the ceiling and covered with hundreds of tiny individual mirrors. When a slow, romantic number is played by the band, the houselights are dimmed and a spotlight with a revolving color wheel on the lens plays across its surface. The huge globe itself rotates. The result in the darkened ballroom is that tiny bits of colored light flash in the darkness and skate all over the interior. It's a striking effect, and I've never tired of it.

As we came in and found a table, the light was playing on the ball. It wasn't hard to find a table. It was too early in the season for crowds. In fact, I was surprised to find a band playing there before the Memorial Day weekend. I looked up at the stage and saw a sign that identified the orchestra playing as Jimmy Di Quisto's Rhythm Riders: Sounds of the Great Bands.

I recognized the name immediately. The band plays at functions that want a nostalgic evening and can't, or won't, foot the bill for one of the famous old-time bands. I have heard the band advertised on the same station that features old music. I explained to Carl about The Rhythm Riders. Surprisingly, he wasn't offended, as I expected a purist to be.

"Makes sense," he said over the music. "After all, the guys who led those great bands are mostly gone or retired nowadays. Certainly not more than a handful of the original musicians remain either. Oh, sure, Count Basie is still playing, but the Dorseys, the Duke, Stan Kenton . . . all gone. If these guys are good musicians and are playing the original arrangements, the way they were intended. . . . Then what's the difference?"

The music stopped just then, and the band went into its closing theme for a few measures, and Jimmy DiQuisto announced in true cliché fashion, "We're going to take a pause for the cause now, ladies and gentlemen. We'll be back in fifteen minutes with a whole lot of your favorites and maybe even ours . . . heh-heh. See you soon!" Big chord from the band, then recorded music floated over the sound system.

A waiter in immaculate linen came up and handed us a wine list and a small menu. The Ballroom carte offered snacks, mostly. An item caught my eye.

"Waiter, this bucket of steamed shrimp-in-the-shell on ice. . . . Is that frozen shrimp?"

You would have thought I'd blasphemed, from the look on his face.

"Oh, no, madam," he said in a rich Spanish accent. "All our seafood is fresh daily! Our shore bucket with lobster and roasted herb corn is Maine lobster, flown in live . . ."

I looked at Carl and he at me. I nodded enthusiastically. Somewhere inside, I heard a distant grunt from my alter ego, Petunia. I should explain. You see, Doris Fein is a sensible young woman, who watches her diet and maintains her decorum. *Petunia* Fein, however, is capable of downing a double banana boat at *Baskin-Robbins* for a snack. Like Doctor Jekyll, I sometimes have trouble controlling her.

"Swell," Carl said to the waiter. "We'll have two shore buckets and a bottle of champagne."

I handed Carl the wine list and gulped at the prices.

I sat in shock as he ordered a bottle of Mumm's Cordon Rouge. The waiter was also impressed. Evidently, not many people ordered it. From the price I knew why. After the waiter left, I said, "Carl, that wine is outrageously priced! Should you have done that?"

"Why not?"

"Well, it's. . . . It's so extravagant!"

"Who eats Maine lobster with Seven-Up?" he smiled. "Besides, this is my first vacation in six years. I've been going to college, then law school year round. This is the first year I haven't had to cough up tuition money for the following fall. But I've saved just as though I had to."

"You should keep on saving," I said. "You never know when. . . ."

"I *do* know when. Right now is when. I'm with someone very special to me, with something very special to say. I feel that lobster and champagne are the only proper accompaniments."

The band came back onto the stage and began to play "Cherokee," the theme of Charlie Barnett's old band. As they did, the waiter arrived with the champagne. He set up a standing ice bucket; showed Carl the label on the bottle. Carl nodded approval and the waiter drew the cork with a moist *plop,* as is proper. He poured a sample for Carl, who again nodded, and then served me. Carl raised a glass.

"Here's looking at you, kid," he said in an excellent Bogie impression. "And here's to us and things to come," he added in his own voice. We clinked and drank.

Uh-oh, here it comes, I thought. He's about to propose marriage to you, I told myself. And what are you going to say? I felt strange. Like most women, I'd had it dinned into my head from childhood that marriage was a legitimate career goal. During my Petunia days, I'd despaired of ever getting an offer. But now, faced with a real proposal, I wasn't sure I wanted it. After all, I was no longer that same lonely fat girl. Though I must admit that, since coming home from Europe, I'd been thinking like the old Doris Fein. It must be living with my family that brings it on. Childhood memories, and all. . . . But I was spared having to answer Carl.

For at that very instant, with a groan of twisted metal and a thunderous crash, the huge reflector ball came smashing down onto the middle of the dance floor!

5/The Casino Has a Ghost

When the ball crashed to the floor, the effect on the Casino Ballroom was devastating. The Rhythm Riders' big band arrangement straggled off into isolated honks and toots, rather than cutting off abruptly. The house was in semi-darkness to allow the reflections of light from the ball to be more effective. A number of the people on the dance floor began to panic. I could see one woman lying inert on the polished wood. A person —I couldn't tell from the hoarse quality of the cry whether it was man or woman—began to scream. That's when Carl acted and took me completely by surprise.

In a second, he vaulted the railing separating the table area from the dance floor. He made straight for where the ball had thundered to the floor. But I noticed that, as fast as he moved, he miraculously seemed to avoid all the broken glass and debris underfoot. No mean feat, considering that the floor was in semi-darkness. The spotlight and color wheel still played over the area high above, where the reflector ball had hung.

Now smaller cries and moans began from the scattered dancers on the floor. Carl rushed to the center of the floor and knelt at the side of the fallen woman. He produced a pocket flashlight on a key chain and, in the spill of its limited light, I saw him thumb back one of the woman's eyelids. I knew he was checking for uneven eye pupil size, an indication of concussion or possible fracture of the skull. I'm not a doctor's daughter for nothing. Evidently satisfied as to the woman's condition, I heard him cry out in a voice so loud and clear that I could hardly believe it was Carl. He's so soft-spoken.

"Lights! Someone turn on the houselights!"

It may have been pure coincidence that the lights came on at that very moment. Or Carl's cries may have finally caused someone at the switch to act. But the effect on the crowd was galvanic. It was as though when Carl commanded light, there *was* light. Carl was in the middle of the dance floor, standing over the body of the fallen woman, in his hand an open folder displaying his New York City policeman's badge.

"Police officer!" he shouted. "All you people near the rail, move back." Turning to the crowd that was beginning to gather around the injured woman, he snapped angrily, "Get away from this woman. Stand back!" The crowds obeyed instantly. He spotted a waiter standing at the edge of the rail, gawking.

"You! Waiter!"

"Yessir?"

"Get me a clean towel and some warm water. Immediately!" The waiter sped off. "You! Bartender!" Carl shouted across the huge room to where the long bar was situated. "Call the police and an ambulance. Right now!"

I watched in awe as Carl turned what might have been a panic into a scene of utter efficiency. All during his visit, I'd thought of Carl as, well, Carl. A nice, handsome, intelligent, and sensitive young man who was essentially a quiet person. It was too easy to forget that he'd been a New York City policeman for six years. And, oh my! How that training showed.

A well-dressed man came out of the crowd toward Carl. Carl turned and growled, "I said to stay off this floor."

"I'm a doctor," the well-dressed man called.

"That's different," Carl said. Then to the crowds around the rail, "Give way! Let that man through. He's a doctor!"

The crowds parted like the Red Sea and, seizing the opportunity, I followed in the doctor's wake. I reached Carl's side at the same time as the doctor, who immediately bent over the injured woman. Carl looked at me for a split second as if to say, What are you doing here? Then, seeing that the panic had been averted, relaxed.

"I think that woman's all right. No sign of concussion. I'm pretty sure she just fainted. Very lucky that no one was directly under that thing when it fell. It must weigh six hundred pounds, easy."

Funny the things that pop into your head when an emergency occurs. I realized that when Carl began raising his voice and giving orders, all of a sudden his New York accent became very, very pronounced. Generally, it has only a suggestion of the traditional argot. But in this moment of stress, he sounded like a bit player in *Godfather II.* For a second, I felt as though I were back in New York when all the terrible things were going on.

The spell was broken abruptly when I glanced over my shoulder. There behind me, towering like a bearded oak, was Harry Grubb. He put a large, gnarled hand on my shoulder. "You all right, Doris?" he asked solicitously.

"I wasn't on the floor when it happened. I'm okay."

Without warning, Carl raised his voice to parade ground level again. "You!" he said, pointing to a couple. "Don't leave the dance floor. I want everyone who was on the floor when it fell to stay here! There'll be questions. There's broken glass all over. Go to the far end of the floor and stay there. Understand?"

The couple who were making their way toward the railing stopped as if turned to stone. They hesitated for a second, then joined the rest of the dancers. Back in the center of the room, the doctor was ministering to the injured woman who was now sitting up with her eyes open. The doctor was dabbing at some cuts on the woman's face with the towel and water fetched by the waiter.

Carl went over to the doctor, exchanged a few words I couldn't hear, then, reaching inside his suit coat, took out a black notebook and a Mark Cross gold pen. He made an entry in the book, then walked to the far end of the dance floor where the huddled knot of shocked dancers had gathered. Harry and I followed. Carl was moving so quickly that even Harry's long legs weren't able to keep pace. I caught up to Carl fully three seconds after he began speaking to the frightened group.

"Now, who was nearest the ball when it fell?" he asked of no one in particular. Everyone in the group looked at each other. No one spoke.

"Come on, come on!" Carl rapped impatiently. "Somebody saw or heard something. This is important. I need your statements while it's all still fresh in your minds."

He scanned the faces of the dancers. "Somebody was dancing with the woman who fainted. Who was it?"

A small, middle-aged man in the back rank of the crowd timidly raised his hand. "I was."

"Over here," Carl commanded. The man approached him. "First, what's the woman's name?" he asked.

"Johansen. Marta Johansen," the frightened man said.

"Address?"

"Sixteen-fourteen Golden West Way, Huntington Beach."

"Is that Miss or Mrs. Johansen?"

"Uh, Mrs."

"You Mr. Johansen?"

"Mmmrble," said the pale-faced man.

"What? Speak up!" Carl said impatiently.

"No. My name is, err, Smith. Yes, Alan Smith."

Carl wiped his face with his hand and said elaborately, "Listen, mac. I don't care what you two were doing here. I don't care a damn about your private life. But a woman's been hurt. You're going to have to tell the truth to the local authorities anyway. You were the closest when that thing fell. Did you have any warning? Did it make any kind of sound before it fell?"

"I want a lawyer," the little man said softly.

"You'll get one, pilgrim," drawled a voice from behind us. "Just answer the man's question."

We all turned. Standing behind us was a stocky gray-haired man in a khaki uniform, semi-cowboy Stetson, boots, and open shirt. On his chest was a gold-plated badge that proclaimed him to be sheriff of Camelot township. His face was florid, and his nose crisscrossed with broken capillaries that bespoke eloquently the sheriff's drinking habits. He wore a pearl-handled revolver in a western-type holster and gunbelt. He looked like the sheriff in *Smokey and the Bandit,* but his accent was pure California.

"I'll take it now," he said peremptorily to Carl. "But you stay here. I don't know who you are, either."

"Suzuki," Carl said, flashing his badge case. "N.Y.P.D."

The sheriff directed his gaze at Harry Grubb and me. "We're with him," I explained. The sheriff favored Harry and me with that look of casual contempt all law enforcement officers seem to be able to muster at a moment's notice.

"Stand over there," he said, waving a hand toward the far railing. "This is police business." He turned and looked back at the dance floor where the reflector ball had fallen. Involuntarily, so did we all.

A man in white uniform was now at the doctor's side. Two others were setting up a gurney. That's the real name for those stretchers on wheels. In a trice, they had the injured woman secure and, extending the wheels, began to roll her toward the exit. "We'll get her statement at the hospital," he said to Carl. "She's in shock right now. Ain't hurt though. Just awful shook up."

"What about lover boy over here?" Carl asked the sheriff.

"We'll get him, too. Down at the station."

The sheriff hitched his trousers up a bit on his pendulous potbelly, and surveyed the dancers, who still looked askance. He ignored them completely and said to Carl, holding out a meaty hand, "Sparky Satterfield. I'm sheriff of Camelot Township. You did a good job there, son. Were you on the floor when it happened?"

"No, just about twenty feet away. I heard the noise, but didn't know what it meant until the ball let go and fell."

"There was a noise *first?*" asked Satterfield. "What kind?"

"Like metal on metal, about to let go. You've heard the sound."

"Yeah, I have. In the war." He unselfconsciously scratched his rear end, oblivious to the fact that every eye in the house was on him. Or maybe he did know, and was signaling his contempt for anyone's opinion other than his own. I sometimes think that's why, at least once per game, you'll see some athlete do it on national TV. And most of the time it's not their rumps that they scratch. He redirected his attention to the crowd and to Carl.

"Say, Suzuki. I'd appreciate your help for a bit. I gotta take statements off anybody near, or who saw it fall. My deputy's a good man but, for writing things up, he's as useful as a bumper on a Sherman tank. Can you split this group with me, pre-interrogate? If we work together, maybe we can all get outa here before the last ferry to the mainland leaves."

"Can do," Carl said, quickly. "We're staying over. At the hotel." The two men then began the tedious process of interrogating any possible witnesses. Harry and I drifted over toward the bar.

"Shouldn't we be staying where the sheriff told us?" I asked.

"Not at all," Harry said easily. "He didn't mean it. That's an old police game. He got here after the action and had to establish that he was the law. The way you do that is to give orders. You saw Carl do it just a few minutes ago. As soon as one person does what you order them to, the rest will fall in line. As long as we don't wander too far, it'll be okay."

Business was brisk at the bar. I guess it was a reaction to what had happened. People were secretly celebrating the fact that they were unhurt. It's a very human response, and it reached me as well. I don't really drink. I may have a glass of wine with my dinner on rare occasions. But once Harry got the bartender's attention, I didn't order my usual Perrier with lime. Harry ordered a cognac and soda, I did likewise.

When the drinks arrived and I picked mine up, I saw that my hand was trembling. I hadn't mentioned it, but before the huge reflector ball had fallen, I was going to forestall Carl's question by dancing. If the champagne hadn't arrived when it did, the ball might have caught Carl and me on the dance floor. I gave another little shudder. Harry noticed it.

"Grim business, this. Lucky no one was seriously hurt. That thing could have killed someone." As if reading my thoughts, he added. "Lucky, too, you and Carl weren't on the floor."

"I thought of that, Harry. Frankly, it scares me."

"Everyone feels that way. I remember the first time I covered a hanging for *The Trib* in Chicago. Back in 1931. Thank God I was with some old hands in the newspaper game. I was ready to bolt from the room. But McCafferty of *The News* was with me and cooled me out." He grinned evilly in recollection. "It would have finished me in the business if I had. Paddy knew that and saved a budding career."

I didn't care for the line this conversation was taking. I'd had enough of death and near death for one day. I artlessly changed the subject.

"I was surprised to see you here, Harry. I thought you'd be off with Mrs. Grayson, or back on the yacht playing gin with Captain Jack."

"Right on both counts," Harry said, sipping his cognac and following it with a sip of club soda. "I dropped Helen off, took the cart to the dock, and played a few games with Jack. But the deck was colder than ice."

"You just dropped Mrs. Grayson off? Just good-night and see you tomorrow?"

"At my age, my dear Doris, one is not as glandular as at yours. I was satisfied with her company on the ride home to her bungalow. Besides, I'm looking forward to that breakfast I was promised."

"I'm sorry," I said, flushing slightly. "I didn't mean that . . ."

"I know exactly what you didn't mean. No offense whatsoever. I only wish that I had something to cause you to apologize about."

It didn't matter. I *was* embarrassed. Silly, I guess. But I don't think of truly older people as being all that interested in sex. Companionship, yes. But I do know that for all his years, nearly eighty of them, Harry Grubb has been a vital, accomplished man. He keeps a pace at *The Register* office that many cub reporters envy. Dave Rose, the editor-in-chief, says that Harry has the energy of a twenty-year-old.

To cover my blushes, I inadvertently took a large gulp of the drink in front of me. It was as though I'd swallowed a half ounce of lighter fluid. With tears in my eyes, I swallowed hard and fought back a temporary wave of nausea.

"Wrong pipe?" Harry asked solicitously. I nodded, with blurry eyes.

"Gotta watch this stuff," Harry said. "It's killed more Frenchmen than two world wars." He glanced at his pocket watch. "Hope they're done soon over there. Once the reports are in, I'll call *The Register* and get my story filed on this."

"Harry Grubb! You'd phone in your own funeral to the paper, if you could!"

"Don't have to," he grinned. "I've already written my own obituary. All rewrite has to do is fill in the particulars of my demise, when it happens. Be damned if I want to be sent off with inept writing by some second-class stringer."

I didn't get a chance to reply to that one. Carl came up to us just then. Harry ordered a drink for Carl and, while we were waiting, began to pump Carl for information about the accident.

You can't blame Harry for the habits of a lifetime as

a crime reporter. He's of the old school. The kind of reporter who interviews a widow and, while she's not looking, swipes a picture of the deceased off the mantel-piece to make the bulldog edition.

"Just a freak accident, was it?" he asked Carl.

"I'm not sure of that, after talking to Buffalo Bill over there," Carl said, indicating Sheriff Satterfield. "It's one too many to be a complete coincidence."

"There have been others?" I asked, my curiosity piqued.

"Half a dozen or more over the past five years."

"Any discernible pattern?" Harry asked.

"Yes and no. Most of it has been along the lines of malicious mischief. Stocks of whiskey in the cellar broken into and bottles shattered. The rental boats they tie up near the Casino were sabotaged. Holes drilled in the bottoms. Power failures during busy weekend nights. Food spoiled in the refrigerators . . . that sort of thing. This is the first time anyone's been hurt."

"Sounds like somebody has it in for the Casino."

"Not necessarily," Carl said. "Satterfield tells me that there are old-time residents on the island who hate the tourist trade. Would do nearly anything to discourage it."

"Doesn't sound right to me," I said. "It's one thing to grouse about the tourist trade, it's something else to endanger someone's life."

"Well, we don't know yet if the ball falling wasn't simply an accident. It's been up there since the Casino opened in the 1930s."

"Don't they have to do a safety inspection on it?" Harry asked.

"They sure do," Carl admitted. "In fact, because this is the first weekend of the season, it was checked out yesterday. And they tested it again this afternoon, before the Ballroom opened."

"And?"

"It was working just fine. But to make sure. . . . Oh, here comes the cowboy," Carl said. Sheriff Satterfield came up and joined us. He accepted Harry's offer of a drink. He ordered a double Jack Daniels and knocked it down like it was Gatorade. He wiped his mouth suavely with the back of his hand and turned again to Carl.

"Well, Suzuki. You ready?"

"Whenever you are, sheriff."

"Okay, but I warn you, it's a rabbit run up there above the ceiling. You take a wrong step, and you could go right through some sections of the overhead."

"I'll take my chances," Carl said. "I've come this far with the investigation, I might as well see it through."

"What's going on?" I asked. Satterfield acted as though I hadn't spoken. Carl replied.

"We're going up above the ceiling to where the fixture is anchored . . . *was* anchored, I should say. Find out what made it fall." He glanced around the huge room, which was now rapidly emptying out. Statements had been taken, and people were hurrying to get the last ferry to the mainland.

"Now where the hell is the house engineer?" Satterfield asked of no one in particular.

I spotted a tall thin man in coveralls headed toward us. "Would that be him?" I asked, pointing.

"Sure is him," the sheriff drawled. "Over here, Slim."

he called. The tall thin man came over to where our party sat at the bar.

"I don't understand this," he said without preamble. "I checked that sucker out yesterday, and it was solid as Gibraltar."

"Couldn't have been that solid, Slim," the sheriff said. "It fell down, didn't it?"

"Are you telling me I don't know my job, Sparky?" said Slim, coloring. "Because I've been chief engineer here for . . ."

"Twenty years," finished the fat sheriff wearily. "We all know you do a good job, Slim. But I gotta look at the fixture base. It's official business, savvy?"

"Then you think the spook done it?" Slim asked, his voice rising.

"I'm not sayin' anything of the sort . . ."

"Just a minute, here! What's this *spook* business?" Harry interjected.

"Nothing, nothing at all. Just a lot of superstitious crap," said Satterfield. "Bunch of things go wrong with a fifty-year-old building, and these damn fools start saying it's haunted."

"Better and better!" Harry Grubb chortled. "Much better story!"

"Hey, wait a minute," Satterfield said, eyeing Harry suspiciously. "Nobody told me you was Press."

"You never asked," Carl put in. "This is Harry Grubb. He's a reporter for *The Santa Amelia* . . ." Carl groped for the name.

"Register," said Harry, producing a press card from his wallet.

"Well, this ain't anything that would interest the papers," Satterfield said belligerently. "Nobody got hurt. Nobody's dead. It was a *accident,* understand?"

"You don't mind if I reserve judgment on that till after the inspection, do you?" Harry said, grinning wolfishly. He smelled a story. I've seen that look on his face before. He wasn't about to be put off.

Thirty minutes later, Carl, the sheriff, and Slim returned. All of them were covered in dust and dirt. Slim had a huge smear of grease on his left cheek. Carl and the sheriff both wore worried expressions.

"Just like I said," Slim said as he came up to us at the bar. "I knew that thing was solid yesterday."

"What made it fall?" Harry asked quickly. The sheriff moved to preclude conversation, but too late. Slim felt his abilities as an engineer had been impugned, and justification was in order.

"*Who,* not what," Slim said. "The support shaft was sawed nearly all the way through. Retainer brackets had all the bolts loosened. It wasn't no spook, either. Not unless spooks need wrenches and hacksaws. . . . Look!"

I noticed then the wrench and small handsaw he held. I hadn't thought of it. You expect to see a man in coveralls carrying tools.

"You found these things up there?" Harry asked, his eyes glistening.

"Yep. And they sure as hell ain't mine!" said Slim.

6/Samurai-Jewish Wedding

I stared at the tools in Slim's hand, fully realizing the implication of his words. Someone had deliberately sabotaged the fixture. It was intended to fall! Harry, Carl, the sheriff, and Slim stood there unspeaking. Then finally Sheriff Satterfield said, "Well, whoever done it ain't up there in the overhead now." He glanced at a Timex on his wrist. "And it's well after midnight. Let's wrap it up for the night."

"Without searching any further?" I asked.

"Lady," the sheriff said heavily, "you don't know much about this building, do you?"

"Only what I've seen. And I know a bit about its history."

"What I know about it, you can't read in books or newspapers." He looked pointedly at Harry Grubb. Then he fell silent.

"Oh, come on, Satterfield," Harry said. "Don't dangle a remark like a carrot in front of my nose, then jerk it away. What about this place?"

"It's honeycombed underneath and above. They didn't name it a casino for nothin', you know. Used to be a full gambling setup downstairs, with all kinds of twists and turns built right in. In case of a raid from mainland authorities, they'd have enough warning to close down before the raiding party could get through the door." He scratched at his rump again. "And that ain't all they had there. Prohibition was still the law when it opened in 1930. All the booze was stored downstairs in rooms that had hidden doors. If you don't know exactly what you're lookin' for, you wander around for a week and never find your way out."

"Surely there's some kind of blueprint or official plan?" Carl inquired.

"Yeah, there is," Slim volunteered. "But it don't mean squat. See, when the Casino went up, there was never anything like it on the island before. That means it didn't have to conform to no existing building code. I mean, what could a building inspector check for? How could he know? All that's on file in Town Hall is the phony plan they used to throw off the Prohibition agents and their axes."

"Back to square one," I said dully.

"Don't you fret yourself, miss," Satterfield said. "This here's a poh-lice matter. We'll take care of it. You just go back to your hotel and get a good night's sleep."

The incredible condescension and male arrogance stung me. Just as though he'd patted me on the head and told me not to strain my poor, feeble, feminine mind with the affairs of hairy-chested men.

"My name is Fein," I said carefully. "*Ms.* Doris Fein. I am not a child. I am a qualified adult person and, for your information, I have done investigative work for the United States government."

"Yep, lady. And I'm Roy Rogers," he said with a sneer. "Don't try to kid this marine. You don't look to be twenty-one yet!"

"She's telling the truth, Sparky," Carl said. "She helped crack a real hush-hush case in New York. That's where we met."

"No kiddin'?"

I was about to say something else, but I caught Carl's cautionary look. I know enough to lay out when I see that look. When we were investigating the disappearance of my aunt and uncle in New York, I ignored that look, and ended up with my foot firmly in my mouth. Carl immediately changed the subject.

"You were in the Corps, huh?"

"Sure was," said the sheriff, warming. "Made sergeant before I got it on Iwo Jima. . . ." His voice trailed off. He'd been about to tell a war story, I'm sure. But he'd suddenly realized the man he was speaking to, his fellow police officer, was Japanese. A silence fell over the entire party. As it did, the waiter who had served us came up.

"Closing down, sir," he said to Carl. "Should I clear away the table?"

My friend Petunia gave an inner howl of protest. With all the excitement, I'd forgotten that we had champagne and lobster back at the table. Carl looked at me.

"It'd be a sin to waste it," I said with a smile. "The champagne is probably flat and warm by now, but cold lobster is good any time."

"How about I put it in a doggy bag?" the waiter inquired.

"Just the lobsters," Carl said. The waiter soon returned with a pair of paper sacks. Carl began to check off items in his notebook with Satterfield. They were going over the list of witnesses and cross-checking the answers they'd gotten during interrogations. I could see it would take a while.

"If you don't mind," I said to Harry and Carl, "I'm going to call it a night."

"Me too," said Harry Grubb. "I've promised a certain lady that I'll be on her doorstep at six this morning." He uncoiled a couple of yards of himself from his barstool and offered me his arm. "Come on, Doris. I'll walk you as far as the hotel."

"You don't have Mrs. Grayson's golf cart?"

"Left it plugged in at the dock. Walked over after that pirate cleaned me at gin."

Harry dropped me off in front of the hotel and went off whistling a tune down the empty streets of Camelot. I've heard of taking in the sidewalks at night. But after the last ferry has left Camelot, you could shoot a canon down the length of Main Street and not hit a soul. The streetlamps weren't of the super-bright type. They were the fancy ironwork sort you see in old flicks, or in model railroad towns under Christmas trees. Each lamp cast circles of yellow light, with small areas of darkness between. From in front of the Camelot Hotel, I watched Harry Grubb alternately appear and disappear down the street. Then I went into the hotel, woke the desk clerk, and got my key.

The room was old-fashioned, with a threadbare rug

over newish vinyl tile. There was a rump-spring double bed, a Grand Rapids escritoire, a mismatched pair of wheezy chairs whose stuffings protested when one sat on them, and a reading lamp next to one of the chairs. The fixtures in the bathroom were equally venerable. The flush tank was of the overhead type I'd encountered in Paris. The bathtub was huge with ball and claw feet. But the water was piping hot from the taps. I used the old-style rubber stopper-on-a-chain to seal the tub and, while it was running, addressed myself to the two doggy bags I'd brought from the Casino. Like they say in New York, I shouldn't oughta have done it. Two cold lobsters don't make for fairytale-like dreams. . . .

I looked down into the polished metal mirror in my hand. The face that looked back was definitely Doris Fein, but the makeup! An elaborate hairdo with a strange tiara-like arrangement of flowers adorned my head. My face was painted dead white with a slash of carmine for a mouth. My eyes were elaborately made up, with blue eye shadow that had flecks of silver. I was made up in classic Japanese whiteface. I glanced down and saw that I was wearing a richly embroidered kimono. I recognized the outfit at once. I'd seen it in a movie.

For years, Larry Small dragged me to every martial arts movie within a fifty-mile radius of Santa Amelia. I'd seen *Samurai,* all six hours of it, at least twice. The outfit I was wearing was a formal Japanese wedding dress. I was kneeling on a *tatami* mat, holding the mirror when a *shoji* screen slid open. My mother came in. She was wearing the same outfit as when Carl and I had dinner with her.

"Are you ready, darling?" she asked. "Everyone's waiting."

In a trance-like state, I rose in a beautiful, fluid motion, realizing it was all a dream. I knew it had to be. The only time I've ever sat on a *tatami* mat was at Carl's Aunt Lucille's restaurant. Then I was mortally embarrassed at all the puffing and groaning it took. I followed my mother out of the Japanese house into the garden. Except it wasn't a Japanese garden. It was the backyard of our home in Santa Amelia.

A pavilion decked with flowers stood at the end of the garden. Folding chairs flanked an aisle that led to a *chuppah,* the traditional Jewish wedding canopy. One side of the aisle was filled with relatives I hadn't seen in years. The other was filled with traditionally garbed Japanese people.

Standing under the *chuppah* along with Dr. Berman, our rabbi, was Harry Grubb as best man. Next to Harry, in the full barbaric splendor of a high-ranking samurai, complete with swords, was Carl Suzuki!

As I walked down the aisle, my father materialized wearing his white coat with an ophthalmoscope around his brow, its mirror flashing light. From somewhere behind me, I heard the strains of Mendelssohn's *Wedding March.* Then as I came up the steps to the *chuppah,* I heard my Uncle Saul begin to sing "We've Only Just Begun." I know that's dumb, but in my dream it all seemed to make perfect sense. Uncle Saul was in excellent voice too.

I reached Carl's side and we exchanged loving glances. Just as Dr. Berman was about to begin the ceremony, a rough, familiar voice cried out from behind me.

"You *dare* to wed this woman?' " it cried.

As one person, the entire assembly turned. A terrifying figure stood at the head of the aisle. Garbed completely in black with drawn sword stood a *ninja!*

If you've never seen a martial arts movie, a *ninja* is the most feared warrior in the world. They dress in black robes with black *tabi,* the split-toed socks that Japanese wear under their sandal thongs. The *ninja* even blacken their hands so they can't be seen in the dark and wear black, hood-like masks that reveal only their eyes.

The *ninja* are assassins, members of a bloodthirsty cult that has brought sudden and silent death to countless thousands over the centuries in Japan. It's said that they can walk up walls, remaining totally motionless for hours, and so seem invisible. They are masters at swords, karate, and *kurisen* throwing. *Kurisen* are star-shaped, razor-sharp steel darts thrown at an enemy. The needle-sharp tips of the stars are dipped in deadly poison!

With a hoarse cry, Carl roughly shoved me to one side and drew his long sword. *"So, desu ka,"* he hissed at the *ninja.* "You dare defile this occasion with your filthy presence. Then know the wrath of Suzuki-Goroh, Lord of Osaka and prince among samurai!"

"Your head will roll, Suzuki-sama," replied the ninja, launching a *kurisen* at Carl. Carl moved a fraction of an inch. The *kurisen* whizzed by him and embedded itself into a post of the *chuppah,* a hair's breadth away from my face.

Carl and the *ninja* began circling each other, feinting with their razor-sharp swords. Steel rang on steel.

"Suuuzuukii!" cried Carl, slashing at the deadly figure in black. Carl's long sword sang through the air, and the severed sword arm of the *ninja* fell to the cement floor of the patio. The assassin gave no scream of pain. He sank to the floor, his eyes like a hunted animal's as he tried to stop the flow of blood with his good hand.

Seeing himself defeated, the *ninja* whipped out his short sword. With a lightning fast move of his left hand, he drove the blade into his own throat. At that second, Carl's sword descended, and the hooded head of the *ninja* rolled across the patio. Carl looked down at the headless corpse and kicked at it with a sandaled foot.

"Ninja dog," he growled. Then, to my horror, he wiped his sword clean on the silk sash of his kimono and sheathed the killing blade. He bent over the severed head and stripped away the *ninja* hood. He had his back to me as he did and, when he held up the head by its hair with a savage cry of triumph, I screamed aloud. In his hand he held the open-eyed, contorted-faced head of Larry Small.

I awoke in a cold sweat at the Camelot Hotel. The sun was streaming through the windows. I looked at my wristwatch where I'd left it on the night table. I had trouble focusing at first, then the reassuring face of my graduation watch swam into view. It read 11:40. I realized in a rush the watch was a Seiko quartz. I thought of my Japanese dream and gave an involuntary shudder.

I performed my morning ablutions, dressed in the same clothes as the night before, and went down to the lobby. I was ready for some breakfast. But definitely not at the hotel dining room. Besides, it was almost lunch-time. I had the clerk ring Carl's room, but there was no answer. I turned to walk away, and the clerk, a different one from last night, called after me.

"Are you Miss Fein?"

"Yes?"

"Got a message for you," he said handing me a slip of paper.

It was a note from Carl telling me that he'd gone ahead to Harry's yacht and would meet me there at noon.

I strolled down the main street which was already crowded with tourists from the first ferry of the day. By the time I reached the docks, I'd been jostled, elbowed, and the left leg of my beige pants suit was smeared with a runny-nosed kid's frozen custard. Chocolate, of course.

Harry and Carl were seated at a table on the cano-pied rear deck of the Parvenu when I came aboard. Carl had borrowed some jeans and a sweat shirt from someplace. The sweat shirt bore the inscription PROP-ERTY OF THE LOS ANGELES RAMS across the front. He had rubber *zori,* Japanese sandals, on his feet. It made me think of my dream. I knew I wasn't going to talk about *that* one with him. He waved cheerily at me.

"Hi, sleeping beauty," he said. "Thought you'd rather sleep than risk one of Ismael's breakfasts. I didn't call you when I got up."

"I don't know where you get the energy," I said. "I feel like I've gone fifteen rounds with Mohammed Ali."

"Late to bed and early to rise, gives you a headache and bloodshot eyes," Harry intoned. "I've been up since milking time."

"How was your breakfast with Mrs. Grayson?"

"Superb, as promised. That's one helluva woman."

"Did you tell her about what happened last night?"

"Only in passing. We had other things to talk about."

"Such as?"

"None of your business, my dear," said Harry with no rancor.

"Can this be the same acid-tongued Harry Grubb I've come to know and love?" I asked. "You're positively mellow today!"

"See what a decent meal can do for a feller?" he said, grinning. "Especially when served by so lovely a lady."

"You're quite taken with Helen, aren't you?"

"You wouldn't understand just how much."

"Try me."

"It would take a long, long time. Did you know that she's played in Chicago? At the old Edgewater Beach Hotel. A classical piano recital."

"She did play beautifully, I recall," I admitted. "A pity about the stroke she had."

"Hardly the end of the world," Harry drawled. "They're doing marvelous things these days with rehabilitation. A stroke doesn't mean that your life is over. Just that you have to be careful, that's all."

"True," Carl chimed in. "Look at J.R. Richard, the pitcher for Houston. He had a stroke, and he's a very young man. Papers say he'll be able to lead a relatively normal life and may even be able to pitch again."

"I hardly feel Helen Grayson wants to do that, in any event," Harry said. Then to me, "Hungry? Ismael is about to insult my tastebuds with what he laughingly calls a club sandwich. Sawed right off the tenderest part of the club."

As if on cue, Ismael materialized with two sand-wiches and two bottles of *Dos Equis* beer, flanked by frost-covered pewter mugs. He set them down on the table and said to Harry, "You got a call from the main-land. He's on hold."

"How long? I've been waiting for that call."

"Few minutes."

"Why didn't you tell me right away?"

Ismael shrugged expressively. "You said you wanted your sandwich right away, too. Which 'right away' do I do first? I ask myself this. Then, I figure, do the first 'right away' right away, then the second 'right away.'"

"I feel like I'm in an Abbott and Costello routine when I talk to you, Ismael," said Harry, getting to his feet.

He headed for the bridge, where he could speak pri-vately on the radio phone. "Be back in a few," he called over his shoulder. "Order some lunch, if you're feeling brave."

Ismael went off to get me some coffee and some cold cereal. Carl and I found ourselves alone for the first time since last night at the Casino. Just before the ball fell.

"Any word about the woman who was hurt last night?" I asked.

"Treated and released. Her boyfriend didn't even stick around."

"A real sweetheart," I said, nastily.

"Just scared of a scandal, that's all. The lady is some-one's wife. But not his. Maybe he's married too. Not an evil man, I think. Just a scared one."

"You'll forgive me if I don't have the proper sympathetic attitude," I said. "To me, marriage is marriage. No middle ground allowed."

"Me too," Carl admitted. "When I go, it's for keeps, or not at all." He gave me a meaningful look.

Ismael arrived and set my bowl of cornflakes in front of me, with a tall thermos carafe of coffee alongside. I busied myself with pouring milk over the cereal. I had the feeling that the marriage discussion of the night before was about to resume. After my dream, it was the last thing I wanted to talk about. I didn't have to do any fancy footwork, though. Harry descended from the bridge. He sat down, took a bite of sandwich, made a horrid face, and gulped down a half tankard of *Dos Equis.*

"The man's a career assassin, I tell you," he said, groaning.

"Business call?" I inquired, changing the subject.

"You could say so. I was checking out some things. Last night, I thought I had seen our sheriff somewhere before. I was right, too."

"Do tell."

"Yep. I never forget a good story. Our friend Sparky Satterfield is quite the feller. It was when he mentioned the Marine Corps that it jogged my memory. This morning, I placed a call to a friend of mine who retired last year from the *L.A. Herald-Examiner.* He remembered Satterfield. Loud and clear."

"Come on, don't play around, Harry," Carl said. "If you've got something to say, say it."

"You take all the fun out of it that way. It's why I'm a reporter. I'm an incurable snoop. I love finding out juicy things, then telling the public about it. Hopefully, in a clean and entertaining style."

"Then would you mind," I said heavily, "telling us in a clean, entertaining style the dirt you've dug up on Sparky-baby?"

"Funny you should ask," said Harry with his wolfish I've-got-a-secret grin.

Harry took another swig of *Dos Equis*, belched discreetly behind a long bony hand, and began.

"First off, he wasn't kidding about the Marine Corps. He was one of the most decorated marines in the Pacific in double-you-double-you two."

"I know," Carl observed laconically. "I almost heard about all the Japs he killed until he caught himself."

"That's not all of it. After the war, he joined the L.A.P.D. He ran up another score of citations for bravery. Again wounded. Retired from the force ten years ago."

"He doesn't look that old," Carl said.

"Aha!" cried Harry Grubb. "Very observant. To most young people, anyone over forty gets lumped in with old folks. But you're right. He did retire early. Under fire, too. It was before the Civilian Review Board was an issue in L.A. . . . Maybe it became an issue because of cops like Satterfield. He was up on charges that he killed a chicano kid during a routine bust."

"Wait a minute," Carl said quickly. "If you've never been out on a beat in uniform, don't start making assumptions. There are parts of New York where a cop's life is on the line every second."

Harry raised his eyebrows. "Young man, I have been a crime reporter for most of my life. Credit me with knowing a bit about urban crime, won't you? I also know a great deal about police procedures. You can't last long in my line of work if you don't get along with policemen. And to a certain extent, understand them."

"I'm sorry. No one who hasn't been on the force really understands," Carl said stubbornly. "And, it seems, least of all the press." Harry's irritation was becoming visible.

"Now that you've properly defended a brother officer," he sneered, "may I continue with my story?"

"I just wanted you to know that a teen-age kid can kill you just as dead as a long-term offender, that's all," Carl said huffily. "I've got a scar ten inches long here." He rolled up his sweat shirt sleeve and displayed a vicious-looking old wound. "I got it from a kid that couldn't have been thirteen years old. Collared him breaking into a parked car. He seemed so scared and defenseless that I got careless."

"But you didn't kill the kid, did you?" Harry asked.

"No, got him with a karate kick. Broke his kneecap and, while he was down, cuffed him with my good hand."

"Well, your *friend* Satterfield doesn't have your sweet, forgiving nature," Harry said sarcastically. "He put a .38 caliber slug between this kid's eyes. And the kid was unarmed."

"I'd have to hear more of the circumstances."

"If you'd stop acting like a delegate from the Police Benevolent Association, I'd tell you the rest."

"Sorry, Harry. Go ahead."

"This wasn't the first time for Satterfield. From what my pal on the *Examiner* tells me, Satterfield was gradually going off the deep end. His teen-age daughter had been attacked and messily murdered by a street gang. He got compassionate leave from the force for six months. During that time, he turned vigilante, and tried to nail the gang members that did it."

"I'll bet he got them, too," said Carl with warmth.

"And then some," Harry nodded. "They weren't worth much when he turned them in. Broken up pretty bad. The department hushed it up. Even the *calloused, unfeeling* press cooperated," Harry said. "Then at the trial, all but one were acquitted. On the basis of the Miranda Case. It seems that friend Satterfield worked over the youths and turned them in without reading them their rights. The confession he sweated out from the weakest link in the gang was worthless. After that, Satterfield went bonkers."

"I can understand it," I said. "Not condone it, but I *can* understand." I got a grateful look from Carl.

"But things kept getting worse. Half a dozen brutality charges. Always against chicano kids these things happened. Finally, he shot one. The kid was unarmed and, incidentally, innocent of the charges Satterfield collared him on. Mistaken identity. Oh, the kid had a record. He just was innocent of that *particular* offense. Had a rap sheet as long as your arm. It was only Satterfield's distinguished war record and his bravery citations from the L.A.P.D. that stifled any further charges against him. He retired early under a cloud."

"That was then. That doesn't mean he can't be a good sheriff in a small town like Camelot, does it?"

"Ah!" Harry exclaimed. "And just how did he become sheriff of Camelot Township? The sheriff before him couldn't handle the rougher crowd that began coming here with the expanded ferry service. One night, he got into a beef with . . ."

"Let me guess," I said. "A bunch of *chicano* kids?"

"On the nose, my dear. The former sheriff was being worked over. The kids had circled him and disarmed him."

"Afraid to use his piece," Carl said reflectively. "You never want to shoot a kid."

Harry nodded. "Exactly. And while he was trying not to use deadly force, as they say, the kids swarmed all over him. Satterfield had retired here on the island and was downtown at the time. He and the old sheriff were friendly. Satterfield waded in. By the time he was done, two of the kids were gravely wounded, and the rest were bent out of shape for months. The old sheriff was badly hurt. The town council named Sparky the sheriff, and he's been sheriff ever since."

"You're describing a man who should get a medal, not the dirt you've been slinging," Carl said heatedly.

"Not the point. Satterfield is well known on this island for his attitude toward the tourists. He despises them. He's often said that if the Casino were shut down there'd never be any trouble in the town. In a way he's right. Out of season, this place makes a graveyard look like an amusement park. No crime. But then again, no people either, save for the year-round residents."

"Then just what are you saying about Satterfield?" I asked.

"I'm saying simply that he has a record of mental instability. That he has killed, many times. That he hates the tourist trade and the Casino. And, further, this spook that's never been caught . . ."

"What about the spook?"

"He's never been caught. And each time something happens, it's our friend Sparky Satterfield who investigates!"

"That's absurd!" Carl said. "You blame every unsolved crime on the cop who tries to solve it? What kind of crap is that?"

"You know damned well what I'm saying, Carl. You just won't admit that another cop would do it. I say Satterfield has already done things that make him a suspect."

I could see Carl was furious. I tried to divert the conversation onto safer ground. "But this is all speculation, isn't it? I mean, no one's accusing the sheriff. We're just playing what-if, that's all." I looked from Harry's face to Carl's. Neither of them was about to budge an inch.

"You may be, but I'm serious," Harry said shortly. "It's the old Latin saying, 'Who watches the watchman?' If a cop goes bad, and he's the head cop on the island, who watches him?"

"I won't listen to this any more," Carl said, getting up. "And I won't stay on this damn boat anymore either. I'm going up to Satterfield's office. I told him that I'd give him all the help I can, and I will."

"Then go!" Harry said sulkily. "Just bear in mind that if I'm right . . ."

"You're not right, and I'm going to prove it!" called Carl over his shoulder.

"How will you do it?" sneered Harry.

Carl stopped at the gangway and called back. "I am a detective, you know!"

"A cop is a cop!" Harry shouted back. Then Carl

stalked off. I wanted to follow, but I didn't think Carl wanted company. I turned to Harry.

"That was truly nasty."

"That was nasty truth," he countered. "But truth just the same."

"You don't really believe all that you said about the sheriff, do you?"

"I'm saying it *could* be so. For Carl to deny the possibility is stupid."

"Well, you could have put it better," I said. "But you had to gloat. You and your Senior Citizen's underground intelligence network. You sit there like some old, skinny spider, in a web of retired informants."

"You've come into my parlor and emerged unscathed."

"I don't know if I have or not," I replied. "In your own way, you extract your payment . . . your pound of flesh."

"Something you could easily spare, my dear."

"That was a low shot, Harry Grubb. And I think you're hateful! I'm going after Carl!"

"Up to you," Harry said, as I began to leave. "But tell him something for me. Privately. You keep it in mind, too."

"What's that?"

"If I *am* right about friend Sparky, and Carl or you finds out that I'm right, well . . ."

"Well what?"

"I don't think that Satterfield, if faced with exposure, would hesitate to kill you both!"

7/A Bit of Local History

Harry's parting shot froze me in my tracks at the head of the gangway. I turned and walked back.

"You're quite serious about this, aren't you?" I asked. "This isn't just a theory at all, is it?"

"Serious as I can be. We've both seen the bizarre things psychopaths can do, while seeming to be perfectly sane in all other respects."

"Say, wait a minute," I said. "I just thought of something. How did you get all this information about Satterfield? It couldn't all have come from your stool pigeon in Los Angeles. He might know about Satterfield's record with the L.A. police. But how about his life here on the island?"

"Right you are. I have another informant. Right here on Santa Catarina." Harry grinned. "A very delightful one, I might add."

"Helen Grayson. I should have known."

"So should Carl have. But when a cop hears someone put the knock on a brother officer, all common sense flies out the window."

I came back to where Harry was sitting, finishing the last of his lunch. "I want to talk to Helen Grayson myself," I said.

Harry shrugged. "Don't see why not. You know her longer and better than I do." He got to his feet. "But, if you're going that way, I might stretch my legs a bit."

"Thereby giving you an excuse to see her again?"

"I don't need an excuse. As of this morning, I have a standing invitation."

I wasn't all that happy Harry wanted to go along. I had the feeling that he was playing a hunch. And when you're asking someone questions, you can't slant them toward your theory. I thought he had done just that when he spoke to Helen Grayson, and I really would have preferred to see her alone. Woman to woman.

Harry and I quickly walked the length of the town and puffed our way up the steep slope of Bison Drive where Mrs. Grayson lived. I smiled to myself at the street name. Calling a street a drive when there are no private motor vehicles on the island is so typically Californian. With or without our automobiles, we retain the nomenclature of the motorcar.

Helen Grayson's cottage at number fifteen Bison Drive was simply a showpiece. Painted bright yellow, with an orange tile roof and tieback curtains at the green shuttered windows, it looked more like a child's playhouse than a dwelling place for adults. The path to the front door was flanked by a superb miniature garden. The door knocker was brass, in the shape of a dolphin. Harry knocked with authority, and Helen Grayson came to the door.

"Why, Harry!" she said with a grand smile, "and Doris too. What a lovely surprise. Come in, come in. I was just about to make a pot of tea. Would anyone care for a cup?"

"Not I," drawled Harry. "I just finished one of Ismael's sandwiches. My stomach won't be ready for anything but Tums for an hour or so."

"I'll have a cup with you," I volunteered. "And some conversation, if you're up to it."

"My dear," she said, walking into the kitchen, "I have unlimited time for conversation. I hardly see a soul. Give an old lady half an opportunity, and you'll get your ears talked off. Just tell me the topic for the day."

"Sheriff Sparky Satterfield."

Mrs. Grayson shot Harry a sad look. "I mentioned that about Sparky in confidence, Harry," she said. "I didn't mean for it to be all over the island today."

"I assure you, Helen," Harry said hurriedly, "that it went no further than Doris and Carl Suzuki. Even then, it was in the context of the sheriff's record with the Los Angeles police force. You wouldn't know of that. But added to what you told me, I'm suspicious. It may be Satterfield who's causing the so-called accidents at the Casino."

"Oh, I can't believe that," Mrs. Grayson said, pouring boiling water into a charming Art Deco teapot. "Sparky isn't the pleasantest of men, but he does his job well. He thinks of himself as a protector of people, not somebody who'd harm innocent folks."

"I was ready to accept that opinion this morning, Helen," Harry said, "but, since I saw you, I've spoken with a friend on the mainland. He told me a lot." Harry quickly recapped all he had told Carl and me on the yacht.

"Oh dear," Helen said, two vertical lines forming above the bridge of her nose. "Now Carl will tell Sparky that you suspect him. This is just dreadful! I never intended that. . . . It was just island gossip, that's all. That's what we do here off-season—talk about each other."

"Not to worry," Harry said easily. "I'm a newsman. Carl doesn't know the source of my information. And Satterfield never will. You ought to know that a newsman would sooner go to jail than reveal his source."

Mrs. Grayson sighed in relief, then brightened visibly. "Shall we have tea in the living room?" she asked.

"That would be lovely," I said. "I didn't have time to admire all the artwork when we came in."

"Oh, it's all reproductions," Helen said, setting up the tea service on a low table in front of a couch. "That lithograph over there is signed by Chagall, but that's it."

The little living room could have come straight out of the pages of a home decoration magazine circa 1939. There was even a Morris chair. If you've never seen one, it's the first of the recliners. It has an adjustable back, but it works by moving a rod, like a beach chair or a patio chaise.

But the focal point of the room was the black Steinway baby grand piano. The keyboard lid was closed but not locked. I flipped it up and idly played a scale.

"I couldn't bear to sell it," said Helen Grayson. "Even if I can't play it anymore. It's such a beautiful instrument. And we had such a hard time getting it over here on the ferry. . . . My, that was five years ago!"

"You were lucky to find a place to live here," I said. "Dad says that, to buy a place on Santa Catarina, someone has to . . ." I broke off in embarrassment. What my father had said was *somebody has to die before you can buy a house on the island.* In the presence of two people as old as Harry and Helen, the remark would have been tasteless.

"I know what they say," Helen said. "But the circumstances were happier than that. I already owned this place. I lived here with my late husband. He was lost at sea in World War Two. He was a Merchant Marine officer."

"I'm sorry," I said.

"About what?" Helen said with a smile. "Ancient history, dearie. Jack and I had ten wonderful months here on the island. Then came the war in 1941. He was needed for his naval experience. One day, he sailed away and . . ." She spread her hands expressively.

"Shortly after that, the island was evacuated by the Coast Guard. Everyone was seeing Japanese submarines off the coast," she said.

"Like burglars under the bed," Harry put in. "More false alarms than anything else."

"So true," Helen said. "But the people were frightened. After the Coast Guard, there was a Marine Corps base, then finally the U.S. Navy. The island was deactivated by the military in 1945. I didn't come back. For years I rented the place to summer people. So don't feel sorry for me, Doris. I have memories here, but all happy ones."

We spent more time on small talk after that. But my mind kept coming back to Satterfield. And Harry's dire warning. I asked Helen about the sheriff's personality.

"He's a violent man," she said thoughtfully. "Such

people have always frightened me. Perhaps I over-stated his dislike for the Casino, though. But I have heard him say that if it burned to the ground he wouldn't mind a bit. Said it would make his job a lot easier. It'd be one less reason for folks to come over from the mainland."

"Do you think his dislike would go as far as sabotage?"

"I couldn't . . . wouldn't say. I've seen him in rages and thought him capable of anything at those times. More tea?"

"Uh, no thanks. I want to go to town. See Carl. He should know about all this."

"He already does," Harry said. "That's why he stalked off in a high dudgeon this afternoon."

"You may be a great reporter, Harry Grubb," I said, "but you'd never be a diplomat. If you had approached Carl calmly and logically with your theory, he would have listened. But you didn't give him a choice. You had to ram your ideas down his throat. And I'm not totally convinced that you're right about Satterfield, either. But, considering what Helen has told us, I feel Carl and I should talk." I got up to leave.

"You can take my cart, if you like, Doris," Helen Grayson said.

"Thank you, no, the walk will do me good. Besides, I want to think."

"As you prefer, Doris. Oh, what's that on your slacks?"

I glanced down at the chocolate smear on my suit. I'd forgotten all about it. I explained how it happened.

"You shouldn't keep wearing it that way," Helen

said. "The stain will set. I have some dry cleaning fluid out in the tool shed. Let me go get it."

"No, no. You stay where you are. I'll get it."

"It should be under the workbench in the shed," she called as I went out the kitchen door.

The back garden was larger and even prettier than the front. The tool shed was actually a smaller version of the cottage. It had windows with curtains and, as I entered, I saw a light switch on the wall. I didn't need the lights. The shed's interior was brightly visible in the spring sunshine.

An antique dealer would have gone bonkers over what Helen had stowed away in that shed. End tables, ash stands, an old Philco floor model radio from the pre-T.V. days. A woman's bicycle with a tag that proclaimed it to be an Iver-Johnson, a brand I'd never heard of before. Or since. Stacks of *National Geographics* and other magazines, dating back to Lord-knows-when. And everything was clean and in good shape. There was none of the dust and debris you'd expect.

I found the can of cleaning fluid. The late Mr. Grayson must have been something of a handyman. There were all sorts of hand tools and electrical gadgets. They were antiques too. All preWorld War Two. The electric motors for the hand tools were bulky and old but, like everything else in the shed, clean and dusted.

I brought the can of cleaning fluid into the house. In a few minutes, we had replaced the ugly chocolate smear with an unattractive circle of discoloration. Somehow, those home dry cleaning things always leave a ring. I thanked Helen for the tea and cleaning off, then got set to leave. Harry made no move to accompany me, so I said my good-byes and headed for town.

When I reached the little Town Hall, Satterfield wasn't in his office. I asked a deputy who was reading a well-thumbed copy of *Sports Illustrated* where the sheriff and Carl could be found. I was told that both were at the Casino. I walked over and got there in time to meet them as they were leaving.

Both men were thoroughly begrimed. Carl's borrowed sweat shirt and jeans were filthy. Satterfield wore a set of dark green fatigues with his name across the pocket and a U.S. Marine Corps insignia below. He had sergeant's stripes on his sleeves. It figured.

"Any news?" I asked.

"Zilch," Carl said. "Sparky and Slim were right. It's like the catacombs in Rome under there."

I accompanied both men back to the sheriff's office, listening more than talking. I couldn't take my eyes off Satterfield. I kept thinking about the violence that waited to erupt from under his facade of the confident, slow-talking law officer. What could trigger that violence? I was curious but, at the same time, I didn't want to find out.

I was relieved when Carl declined the sheriff's offer of a drink or two at the hotel bar. He headed toward the Town Hall. Carl and I strolled toward the hotel.

"Are you staying over another night?" I asked.

"I promised that I'd help Sparky," Carl said. "I figured it wouldn't matter. I can get the last ferry after the Casino shuts down."

"Alone?" I croaked. "Wait a minute. You're not angry with me too, are you?"

"No, of course not," he said. "Oh, you mean, why take

the ferry? Well, Harry Grubb and I aren't speaking just now . . ."

"Don't be foolish," I said quickly. "Harry's not angry. He just rubs people the wrong way sometimes."

"You have a mastery of understatement."

"Well, I don't want to defend Harry Grubb's attitude," I conceded, "but, you must admit, what he said was in your interest. He cares about what could happen to you."

"I lived a long time before I ever knew Harry Grubb. I was a cop, and a good one. I think I'm capable of taking care of myself, Doris."

"Nobody said you couldn't. But you should know what else I learned about our sheriff after you left."

"Oh? Did Harry get another call from his spies?" Carl asked bitterly.

"Not unless you count Helen Grayson as one of his spies. I had tea at her cottage a while ago. That's where Harry got all the local dope on the sheriff. From Helen."

"She'd have no reason to lie," Carl admitted grudgingly. "What did she have to say?"

I filled him in. He nodded and said, "It makes sense. But none of this is evidence. Not even circumstantial. It's rumor and hearsay. The last I heard, a man is innocent until proven guilty."

We entered the sad lobby of the Camelot Hotel. Carl inquired about his suit at the desk. It would be waiting in his room, he was told. He started for the stairwell and suddenly put a palm to his forehead.

"Forget something?" I asked.

"Remembered something. I had my suit cleaned, but

I forgot about my shirt. It's filthy. Listen, Doris, will you do me a favor?"

"Anything."

"Anything?" he asked with a perfectly innocent attempt at a leer.

"Well, *almost* anything," I replied, playing the game.

He reached into his pocket and produced a flat, folded stack of bills. He extracted a twenty and handed it to me.

"Would you take this and buy a shirt for me?" he asked. "I want to hit the showers. A short-sleeved shirt will do. Collar is fifteen-and-a-half. If you get long sleeves, the length is thirty-four."

I laughed. "Try buying a long-sleeved shirt at a California resort area. Any preference as to color?"

"Anything at all, so long as it's white or pale blue."

"Another tough order." I smiled. "I'm sure I can get you magenta or even Haiwaiian prints. But blue or white? I'm not promising a thing."

I located a men's shop and, oddly enough, had no trouble finding exactly what Carl wanted. True, the clerk had to climb a ladder to a seldom-used top shelf. And the box from which he took the shirt had a light coating of dust. I think the shop got as much call for white shirts as it did for buggy whips. The whole transaction took only minutes. I knew Carl would still be showering, so I decided to browse around.

I was walking past Town Hall when I saw a little storefront I hadn't noticed earlier. The gold-leaf sign read SANTA CATARINA HISTORICAL SOCIETY. I peered inside the window at the sepia-toned photographs of the island at various stages of its history, then went in.

A small man, who appeared as old as the island itself, emerged in response to the bell that rang when I opened the shop door.

He wasn't even my height, and dry as a stick left to bleach in the seaside sun. He wore a white, short-sleeved shirt. In a flash I knew why that men's shop carried them. They had at least one customer for the shirts living on the island. He had a gaucho tie at his throat, secured by an ornate turquoise-and-silver ring. His trousers were Western-style whipcords held up by an equally flashy turquoise-and-silver buckle.

I expected him to be wearing boots but, incongruously, he had on rope-soled boat shoes. He looked like a cowboy who got lost at a marina. As he approached me, he arranged his deeply tanned face into a smile that began at his chin and wrinkled its way up to his retreating hairline.

"Howdy," he said in a surprising bass-baritone voice. "What can I do for you today, ma'am?"

"Just browsing around. I thought I might pick up something more than postcards from a tourist-trap store. Something more . . . uh . . ."

"Historical?" suggested the wrinkled little man.

"Exactly."

"Well, you sure came to the right place," he said, his face lighting up. "People don't seem to care about history nowadays." He gave me a sideways look. "Least of all, folks your age. All they want is T-shirts with dirty words on them."

He launched into a semi-diatribe about how no one cared for tradition anymore. He began pointing out views of the island which lined the walls of the little shop, and calling off names of early settlers and island society. I half tuned him out until I heard him saying, ". . . Kellers, Ramseys, the Graysons . . ."

"I beg your pardon. What did you say about Grayson?"

"One of the earliest families. Oh, not old as the Mexican families. But definitely before 1900. The Graysons have lived on the island longer than I have, for sure. And I opened the shop here after the war."

I could tell from the way he pronounced 'the war' that he meant World War Two. Most people his age say those words as though there hadn't been scores of wars since then.

"Helen Grayson is a friend of my family's," I volunteered.

"Really?" the little man said brightly. "Helen's a marvelous woman." He extended a hand. "I'm Charlie Arthur. Curator of the Historical Society, and official island historian. I'm also the village idiot this season. You see, the town's so small we can't afford a full-time idiot. We have to take turns." He broke into a high, cackling laugh. I forced a smile at his dreadful joke.

"Same for the town drunk too?" I asked.

"Sure is. But everyone wants *that* job!" He made a sound like a hen laying a square egg.

"So you know Helen, eh?" he continued.

"Yes. I was just at her cottage. Lovely place."

"Isn't it, though? Close enough to the center of town for shopping, but far away from all these damned tourists. She could sell that cottage for a fortune. But she says she'll probably die there, like all the rest of the Graysons."

"Well, her husband didn't," I said. "He died at sea in the war."

"Husband? What husband?" Charlie asked quickly.

"Jack Grayson."

"Now how in hell could Helen have a husband named Grayson? Unless maybe she married a cousin. Her father's name was Grayson. He built that cottage right after the big house burned down, and before he built the Grayson mansion in 1927. 'Course, the Wrights own the Grayson Mansion now. No, the only way Helen could have a husband named Grayson, she had to marry a cousin."

My head was spinning. Then it came back to me. Helen had never said her husband's name was Grayson. She had called him Jack. I shrugged. It probably had a simple explanation. Helen had readopted her maiden name after her husband had died in the war. She'd mentioned that they had been married for only ten months.

I thanked Charlie for his time and bought a book titled *First Families of Santa Catarina*, authored by— you guessed it—one Charles Evans Arthur. I was going out the door when he called after me.

"You know? Helen probably took up her maiden name when her husband died. I didn't know her until after the war. Yep, she could have been married."

I nodded and headed back for the hotel. Some things were floating around in my mind. Nothing solid, but I did want to speak to Carl.

8/Fire!

It wasn't fated to be. In the same way something kept coming up when Carl tried to talk to me the day before, so did things happen to me. The first happened when I brought Carl his shirt. He was already out of the shower when I got there but still inside the bathroom. His room door was unlocked so I went in. Just as he came out of the steamy bathroom wearing nothing but a preoccupied look, I let out a yelp and turned around. He grunted in surprise and leaped back inside the bathroom. I heard an outburst of Japanese that had to be swear words.

"What's wrong?" I called through the door.

"I slipped and hit my knee on the———bathtub!"

"Are you hurt badly?"

"No, just a bruise. Hang on a second."

Carl emerged again, this time wearing a towel around his waist and a sheepish grin. "Sorry if I shocked you," he said. "It's not like a Japanese bath. We go in for mixed bathing." He sat down in the chair opposite me.

"More surprised than shocked. How's your knee?"

"I'll live. Did you find a shirt?"

"Sure did. Look." I took out the shirt and began removing the pins from it. And neatly ran one under my fingernail. I let out a cry and jumped to my feet. So did Carl, losing his towel. He recovered quickly.

"Sorry. Again."

I laughed. "Look at this. I'm bleeding like . . . oooh, quick!" I tossed him the shirt I had almost bled on. He fielded it expertly and, in the process, nearly lost his towel again.

"This is getting silly," Carl said. "Why don't you go to your room and rinse that pinprick off and bandage it? I'll get dressed and be with you in a few minutes."

"Whatever you say," I said with a nasty grin. "I was thinking of sticking around to catch your next strip-tease act."

"Never mind, lascivious wench," he said, steering me to the door. "I've been trying to tell you for two days that my intentions are honorable."

I went halfway out the door and popped my head back in. "Peekaboo!" I cried. Carl ducked behind the door and threw the damp towel at my head. "All right, all right," I grumbled. "I can take a hint."

I went to my room, cleaned up the pinprick under my fingernail, and discovered that it had already stopped bleeding. I didn't need a Band-Aid. Just as well. There wasn't anything in the medicine chest but sixteen coats of old paint and a cracked glass shelf.

I went down to the lobby and walked right into Satterfield.

"How do, Miss Fein," he said. "I'm afraid we got off

to a bad start last night. Carl's been tellin' me all day about how helpful you was to him in New York. That U.N. affair, I mean."

I let that pass. I didn't want to point out that it was I, not Carl, who had cracked the Dakama case for the I.G.O. In fact, when the mastermind of the plot was captured, I was there. Carl was at Kennedy Airport at the time, chasing down a false lead.

"I do my humble best, sheriff," I said, smiling.

"Can't expect more of a feller than that," said Satterfield. He looked over my shoulder at the stairway I'd just descended. "Here comes the sleuth now," he said. And to Carl, "How's it going, Hawkshaw?"

"I suspect a left-handed, middle-aged man in a dirty raincoat," Carl said.

"I suspect an *any*-aged man in a dirty raincoat," Sparky grinned. "But I was talking about our spook."

"That's different," Carl replied. "Anything new since I saw you?"

"The Astros beat the Dodgers. Three to zip."

"Serves the Dodgers right for leaving Brooklyn," Carl said as we headed out of the lobby. "There's no statute of limitations on treason, you know!"

There were already crowds of people headed for the Casino. It had been a glorious day and now, at dusk, it seemed everyone on the island was bound for the old building. The doors were opened on schedule but, as the Casino is so huge, the hundreds of people barely filled a quarter of the tables. There was something new added, though.

A large section of the dance floor, the spot where the reflector ball had landed, was newly sanded and somewhat lighter in color. The crew must have worked all through the night and day to repair the great gouge in the dance floor. I looked up at where the ball had been.

"Don't know if they can repair the ball," said Satterfield, answering my unvoiced question. "They sure as hell can't replace it. I don't think they make those things anymore. Leastways not that big."

"Good-sized crowd," Carl said.

"This is nothing," Satterfield said. "Wait till Memorial Day weekend. They gonna be jammed in here like sardines. Glenn Miller's band gonna be here then."

"These guys aren't that bad," said Carl, indicating the Rhythm Riders, who were setting up on stage.

"No, they're all right," Satterfield concurred. "But Jimmy and the boys don't have the name. It's the Miller name that draws the crowd. Or any big name. Don't matter that the old guys are long dead. We get a big crowd for the Jack Jameson band too. That's why the boys play so much of his stuff."

As if on cue, Jimmy DiQuisto gave the band a downbeat and they began playing the Miller arrangement of "String of Pearls." I spoke to Carl over the music.

"I don't know the Jack Jameson band," I said. "Were they big?"

"Not as big as the Dorseys or Benny Goodman. They were a West Coast outfit. Very big in Los Angeles at the Palladium. But you must know their recording of 'Deep In a Dream.' It was Jameson's theme song."

"I remember hearing it on KGRB's golden oldies shows."

"Yeah, they play his stuff on New York radio stations too."

"Wait'll the midnight show then," Satterfield said. "On Saturdays, they got the same routine. First show is called 'Tribute To Glenn Miller,' then they do Tommy Dorsey, Jimmy Dorsey, and the last show is 'Tribute To Jack Jameson.'"

"Sort of spooky, though," I said. "They're all dead now."

"We all die," said Satterfield. A shadow crossed his face. Perhaps he was thinking of his daughter. I saw a slow tic begin at the corner of his left eye. He stood up abruptly.

"You'll excuse me?" he said. "I'm going below to check out the basement. Make sure we ain't got any uninvited guests."

A waiter, the same one as the night before, came up to our table. I thought of my nightmarish Samurai-Jewish wedding dream from the lobster. Now that it was long over, it seemed funny. Carl caught my smile.

"Something?"

"Just an inside joke," I said.

"Speaking of inside, how about something for the inner Doris? Are you hungry?"

I heard Petunia mumble something, but bravely I said, "Maybe just a teensy shrimp salad. Oil and vinegar dressing." Petunia's words became clearer: shrimp Louie! she grunted, shrimp Louie! "And a Perrier water with a piece of lime," I added.

I won't tell you what Petunia's rejoinder to *that* was. Carl ordered a steak, salad and, darn him, a baked potato with sour cream.

Dinner was as good as the night before, I guess. I watched Carl eat enough to put me into a new dress size. But I virtuously declined so much as a breadstick. I had black coffee after dinner. Carl had baked Alaska. I could have hit him. After dinner, we danced a bit.

As we moved across the dance floor, involuntarily I glanced up at where the big reflector ball had hung. I noticed several other couples doing it too. It suddenly occurred to me why the crowds were heavy. The news of the accident the night before. I was sure that *The Register* had carried the story. Harry had radiophoned it in. I mentioned my suspicions to Carl. He agreed.

"They want to see where it happened," he said. "I don't know why people are so bloodthirsty. Same as the worst problem at car accidents where you're always keeping the crowds away and traffic moving. They slow down to a crawl. I think they're secretly hoping to see some blood."

"And secretly glad it didn't happen to them," I added.

"Well, we both saw it happen, and I saw you looking up there," he said, nodding at the ceiling. I was about to answer when a disturbance broke out at the main entrance to the ballroom. I saw the crowd shift like a many-headed animal. People began to drift toward the source of the disturbance.

Carl didn't hesitate for a second. He reached inside his coat pocket and took out his badge holder. He clipped it to his breast pocket with practiced ease and loped toward the main entrance. I followed at a more discreet pace.

When I got there, it was almost all over. There were two young men sitting on the floor. One had his head between his hands and was rocking back and forth, in obvious distress. The other sat dazed with blood streaming from a cut at his hairline. Standing over them, with a blackjack in his hand, was Sparky Satterfield! He prodded the dazed youth with a boot.

"On your feet, punk!" he rapped. "Your partyin' 's over, boy."

I came up alongside Carl and whispered, "What's it all about?"

"They tried to smuggle a couple of bottles of booze inside with them," Carl said softly. "Didn't want to pay the prices they get here for a drink, I guess. The doorman spotted the bottles and tried to turn them away. They gave him some lip, and a shoving match began. That's when Sparky showed up."

"That boy is bleeding!" I protested.

"The sap must have broken the skin when Sparky hit him with it."

"Don't call that boy names."

"No, no. The blackjack. It's called a sap."

"Oh."

The youth Satterfield had nudged with a boot didn't react. The sheriff grabbed him by the long hair on his head and hauled him roughly to his feet. A soft oooh! rose from the crowd of spectators.

"Dammit, when I say move, you *move,* boy!" Satterfield said as he handcuffed the youth.

At this point, the other young man, the one with the vacant gaze, fell forward onto his face. It was then I noticed a trickle of blood from his left ear. I grabbed Carl's arm. "That boy has a fractured skull," I said quietly. "He's bleeding from the ear. Don't let the sheriff manhandle him."

"Don't interfere," Carl said softly. "The kid shouldn't have done what he did. Especially with Satterfield on the set. He was committing a crime when Sparky intervened. Attacking an employee of the Casino. If he'd have hit the doorman with a bottle and killed him, what then?"

"But to use a blackjack that way!"

"What would you have him use with two kids that size? Sweet talk? He didn't draw his pistol, you notice. That would have been undue force. No, Sparky's a rough cop. But he's a good one."

I heard the sound of the island's one ambulance approaching. In a few minutes, the unconscious youth was strapped into a gurney. It seemed unnecessary, but before Satterfield let the attendants take the boy away, he handcuffed the kid to the gurney.

"Now that was unnecessary," I said to Carl.

"You don't know that, either. Sparky's no doctor. The kid could be playing possum. Waiting for a chance to get away, or have a go at Sparky."

Carl turned from me and raised his voice to the crowd. His New York accent became stronger as he spoke.

"Awright, awright. That's it, folks. Disturbance is over. Go back to your dancing. Have fun. No trouble here. No problem."

The crowd didn't move. One man called from the back. "Okay, Charlie Chan, okay!"

I saw the look on Carl's face, and it was like the dream of the night before. But if I expected a samurai charge into the crowd and for Carl to go after the offender, I was wrong. Carl gritted his teeth, took a deep breath, and said in a very loud voice, "I said to clear off! If anyone wants to spend some time in a cell instead of dancing . . . that's okay with me, too." He made a move toward the crowd, and they melted away like snow-flakes in a sauna. The band began to play.

"Still feel like dancing?" I asked.

"Not awfully."

"Nobody likes to dance awfully."

"I don't know about that," Carl said, indicating a couple struggling ineptly across the floor. "But if I run into that dude who called me Charlie Chan . . ."

"I see your point. Let's sit a bit. I wanted to talk, anyhow."

We made our way back to our table. I didn't hesitate this time. I plunged right into what Helen Grayson said about Satterfield. I also stressed that I didn't entirely agree with Harry Grubb's theory about the sheriff. Carl listened, his face impassive. Finally he said, "Funny. I didn't think you wanted to talk about Sparky at all. I kind of hoped that you'd want to pick up the conversation we were having last night. Before all this business began."

"I do, Carl. I truly do. But this is hardly the time or place."

"Because you really don't want to talk about it," he said thinly. "No matter."

I could see he was hurt, and I could have bitten my tongue for saying what I did. First there had been the slur by that fool in the crowd. Now, here I was turning him away. But, through it all, I had this feeling I couldn't shake. Of something I may have noticed, but somehow didn't interpret properly.

"Carl, let's begin again," I said with a smile. "We'll have a few laughs and, if you're not up to seeing Harry Grubb, we'll take the ferry back. Uh-oh!"

"What's wrong?"

"My parents. I didn't call them. This has all happened so fast."

"I know what you mean," Carl said. "I called the mainland this morning to ask about my uncle."

"You gave him the sword?"

"Oh, yeah. And he gave me a message for my father. Uncle Jiichi is a tough old bird. He may fool the doctors yet. I had expected to see him in the hospital, but he was at home."

"That may not mean much," I said. "Often when a case is really serious, they send the patient home. That way, he can be in familiar surroundings when . . ." I didn't have to finish. Carl knew.

"I thought of that," he said sadly. "I was worried about him being there alone. But he's strongly connected at the Buddhist temple. He's got a bunch of ladies that take turns visiting him and seeing to his needs. All members of the congregation. Then there are all his students from the *dojo.* He used to teach *kendo.* He doesn't lack for attention. But I know what he'd really like. He'd like to see his son. My cousin Alvin."

"Nobody knows where he is, you told me."

"Now they do. When I called, the lady who answered said he's been located."

"Where has he been?"

"Japan, then San Francisco. He's changed his name. That's why the family had trouble tracing him."

Carl turned in his chair and looked around the room.

"Something?" I asked.

"Nothing, I guess. It must have come from the kitchen. I thought I smelled smoke. Maybe it's heartburn from all the folks who ate tonight at the Camelot Hotel."

The Rhythm Riders broke into a fanfare and Jimmy, the leader, came to the microphone. "And now, ladies and gentlemen," he intoned, "for the midnight show. . . . A tribute to Jack Jameson and his orchestra. Remember this one? The band began the opening strains of "Deep In a Dream." The music swelled and then the lights dimmed. There was no reflector ball to add to the romantic darkness but, in short order, the dance floor in front of the stage was filled with couples swaying to the languorous strains of the Jack Jameson theme. Then it happened.

"Fire!" someone yelled. "The place is on fire!"

This time, even I smelled the smoke. And it wasn't coming from the kitchen. I pointed to a well-lighted area above the bar and said to Carl, "Over there. It's coming through the ventilator duct."

From somewhere inside the building, an alarm bell began to ring. As if in answer, the hoot-hoot of the fire emergency call began to sound from the fire station next to Town Hall. It triggered a panic on the dance floor.

Like a swarm of insects, the crowd on the floor swept toward the main entrance of the ballroom. I began to move that way too. Fire is a scary thing. Carl took my elbow.

"Not that way," he said. "We'll take a fire exit. That's what they're for."

We made our way through the smoke, which was

now visible in the air, to a side door. "See?" he said. "Nothing to it." He pushed on the bar that would open the door. And pushed again. Nothing happened. He grabbed me and dashed for the next fire door, twenty feet away. I saw him hit the door latch with his shoulder. Nothing!

I looked around and saw the same scene being repeated at half a dozen fire exits around the room. They were all jammed shut!

9/No Sawdust on the Floor

"Stand back from the door," Carl said. I moved away. He took two steps backwards and with a cry, launched himself through the air at the jammed fire door, feet first. There was a tremendous thump and the sound of splintering wood. The door flew open and fresh air rushed into the room; Carl spilled out onto the board-walk. He scrambled to his feet immediately.

Without hesitation, he was sprinting down the board-walk to the next fire door. I followed and got there in time to see him prying at the door's far corners.

"Wedges," he said. "Somebody's driven wedges into the doors!" He stood crane-like on one foot. I had no idea what he was going to do. He took off a shoe. Then, using the heel of his shoe for a hammer, he knocked the wedges loose. The door flew open, and a red-haired woman came bursting out. Behind her, I could hear someone crying, "Here's an open one. Over here!"

Carl worked his way down the building, knocking the wedges loose. In a short time, the doors on that side of the building were open, with people in various states of disarray pouring out. It was about this time that the fire engine arrived from town. As I watched it arrive, I also saw Sparky Satterfield come up the boardwalk toward us. He waved to Carl.

"Some mess," he said as he reached us. "And a setup too. No fire down there. Bunch of rags in a container. Lotta smoke, no real fire. It was right near the fresh-air intake ducts, though. That's why the Casino filled up so fast."

"That's only part of it, Sparky," said Carl holding out one of the wedges he'd dislodged from the fire doors. "The doors were wedged shut from the outside."

"That tears it!" Sparky said. "This ain't mischief anymore. I call it attempted murder!"

"We have one break," Carl said. "The wedges themselves. They're all uniform size. Handmade from the look of them. We know more about our spook now."

"You think it's someone with carpenter's tools, or a berserk carpenter?" I asked.

"Definitely someone with access to a carpenter's shop. There were three of these wedges in each door." Carl leaned back and counted from where he stood. "I cleared six doors on this side. Were the other doors jammed? The ones on the other side?"

"Whole place was bottled up tighter than ticks on a hound," Satterfield replied.

One of the ambulance attendants I had seen earlier when Satterfield had beaten up on the two young men came down the walk toward us. He spoke to the sheriff.

"Sheriff, we got a bad one out there. A woman. Severe crushing injuries. She got trampled underfoot in the panic. Gotta get her to the mainland soon as possible."

"Want me to commandeer a ferry?" Satterfield asked.

"I think a boat will be too slow for her. Can you call a chopper on your radio?"

"Can do. Come on, I gotta get to my office! Suzuki?"

"Can I help?" Carl asked.

"You sure can. Take over for me here. My deputy is at the front entrance, moving traffic. He's doin' his best, but that ain't a whole lot. Trouble is, we don't know what we're looking for. Any of the people inside could've done it, hired help at the Casino. We gotta screen 'em all tonight."

"Sheriff, we got to hurry," protested the ambulance man.

"Line 'em up and check their whereabouts all day today," Sparky said. He turned and walked briskly away with the ambulance attendant at his side. Over his shoulder he called, "Be sure to check their hands . . . all of them. We could get lucky if you're right about woodwork."

"What did he mean?" I asked Carl.

"Anyone who's recently cut that many wedges might have also cut his hands, or got a splinter or two. Carpenters have a saying that a job isn't a good one unless there are a few drops of blood on it."

"Grisly motto."

"But true. It isn't just do-it-yourselfers that pinch their fingers or hurt themselves. It happens even to pros."

I followed Carl down the walk to the front entrance.

He quickly organized a screening line of patrons and hired help. He began checking hands and alibis. I drifted off inside the big lobby. I couldn't be of help in questioning those people.

I was idly inspecting the photographs on the wall when I saw what had been bothering me for hours. I examined one yellowed print more closely. There was no doubt of it. And I knew right then who the "spook" could be.

I should have let Carl know where I was going, but he was much too busy interrogating. Besides, I wasn't one-hundred-percent certain of my theory. It seemed so outrageous. My head was buzzing with ideas as I went back inside the ballroom, crossed the empty floor, and took a fire exit door.

As the door swung outward, I heard a smallish thump. Somebody had been standing in front of it, outside. I carefully eased around and I found myself face to face—well, face to collarbones—with Charlie Arthur.

"What are you doing here?" we said simultaneously.

"Watching all the excitement," Charlie said replying first. "I am the official town historian, you know. This here is real news. Something I can write up."

"You wouldn't have been around here earlier, would you?" I asked.

"Nope, spent the day at the Historical Society. Came up when the fire alarm went off. Were you here when it happened?"

"Inside," I said, nodding. "The fire doors were wedged shut. A woman was critically injured."

"Dreadful. Just dreadful," said Charlie, looking like a crestfallen cowboy gnome. "Had to be the spook, then."

"You know about that?" I cried.

"Anyone on the island knows about the spook. Anyone who's lived here for the past five, six years. That's when it all began. Everyone who lives here year round got a theory about it too."

"You included?"

"I got the one that makes the most sense," Charlie replied.

"Do you really?" I said, walking toward town. He followed. I was puzzled about something. "Aren't you going to stick around to investigate for the Historical Society?" I asked.

"Already did. I found out about the doors being wedged shut. I was checking one of them out when you opened it. You hit me, you know."

"And I *am* sorry," I said. "But who told you about the wedges?"

"The sheriff. His office is right next to the Society. When all the noise broke out, I was still at the place doing some research. I met Sparky and Eddie coming down to the sheriff's office. They filled me in."

"Eddie?"

"Eddie Winslow. Owns the ambulance and oxygen service here in town."

"You mean that the ambulance is private?"

"Oh, yeah. Town can't afford it. But Eddie does all right. Lot of retirees here on the island. Seems he's always bringing them into the doctor. Myself, I'm going to outlive them all. I'll be seventy-eight this coming November."

"Really? You don't look it," I lied.

"Clean living. One drink a day. That's all I take."

We reached Main Street and Charlie began to walk

toward Town Hall. I stopped and asked, "Aren't you going to tell me about your spook theory, Charlie?"

"Oh, that. Sure. It has to be somebody from off the island."

"What makes you so sure?"

"None of this stuff goes on when it's off-season, that's why. It has to be somebody who comes over on the ferry."

"It couldn't be a regular resident?"

"Don't be silly. I know every soul on this island. Some of them may grouse about the tourists, but there ain't a one would do this."

"How so?"

"Listen, you hurt the Casino, you hurt the island. We get all our tax revenue from sales taxes. Pays the freight for the whole year. No, it has to be someone comes over from the mainland. Just maybe, and I say maybe, could be one of the summer people who rent for the season. But they come and go. And there's only one summer person who's been here every season something happened."

"Who is that?"

"Glen Markham. And he sure ain't the spook."

"What makes you so sure?"

"He's eighty years old and blind as a bat. Got eyeglasses like the bottoms of milk bottles. No, it's an off-islander doing it."

"Back to square one," I said.

"Beg your pardon, miss?"

"Just thinking out loud," I said. "Thanks for your help and your theory, Charlie."

"Think nothing of it. Most folks don't," he said and

broke into his high-pitched cackle. He walked off toward Town Hall, humming a tune to himself. It was an old song, but I recognized it: "I'm Always Chasing Rainbows."

I didn't stop off at the hotel. I had to check out what I had seen on the wall at the Casino. When I came abreast of the marina, I saw lights in the saloon of the Parvenu. I went aboard. Harry Grubb was in the middle of a very vocal gin game with Captain Jack. Harry was making some reference to Jack's ancestry as I rapped on the open doorway of the saloon.

Harry had his back to me. Captain Jack saw me standing in the door and said to Harry, "Watch your mouth, sore loser. We got lady-type company."

Harry turned and saw me. "Come in, don't stand there like a marine, blocking the passageway."

"I'm surprised to see you here," I said, taking a chair at the card table. "I thought for sure you'd either be at the Casino checking out the fire or with Helen Grayson."

"Right on both counts," Harry said, shuffling the cards. "I've already called in the story. Got it directly from the bridge." He pointed to the deck above. "I couldn't get close enough to the Casino once the fire equipment arrived. They blocked it off. I picked up what I could from the brave fire laddies once the emergency was over. Then I came back here. I was cranking up the ship-to-shore when I heard the radio traffic coming from Satterfield to Point Pleasant Hospital and the Cortez Bay Police helicopter. I just listened in and even got the name of the woman who's been injured. Then I called it all in to *The Register.*"

"What about Helen Grayson?"

"Not feeling well. She felt out of sorts this afternoon. I left her not long after you did. Told her I'd look in on her before we left tomorrow."

"Tomorrow?"

"You didn't think I'd leave tonight with a story like this cooking, did you?"

"I have to call my parents."

"Help yourself," Harry said, ordering the cards in his hand. "Do you know how to work the radio phone?"

"I'm afraid not."

"I'll give you a hand, Miss Fein," Captain Jack said, getting up. "It ain't hard. You'll get the hang of it right away. Just got to turn on the transmitter, that's all." He went to the ladder leading up from the saloon to the bridge, then he stopped. He went back to the table, and he picked up the gin hand that Harry had dealt. With a knowing look, he put the ten cards in his pocket.

"Thanks for that vote of confidence," Harry said sarcastically. "Do you really think your employer would cheat you?"

"Nope. Just don't believe in tempting folks, that's all." Captain Jack started up the ladder with me behind him. At the top, he called back to Harry, "I left the rest of the deck. Don't you touch it."

"How do I know you don't have another deck of cards up there?" hollered Harry from below.

"Because I don't have to cheat to beat you," replied the Captain in a voice that could cut through a heavy fog. "You're my pigeon. One day, I'll own this floating hotel."

Captain Jack showed me how to turn on the transmitter and reach the mainland operator. I waited for a few minutes while my call was patched into the regular telephone lines. Happily, Mom answered.

"Doris! Are you all right, baby? We were so worried. We saw the story in *The Register.* About the reflector thingie falling. Then we got your message . . . Well, we didn't know what to think!"

"I'm perfectly fine, Mom," I said and went on to explain the events of the past thirty-six hours. I didn't dwell on the spook idea. I told her I thought it a series of coincidences. No point in worrying her unduly. I also told her that I'd been seeing Helen Grayson. She said to send her regards to Helen.

"I often wondered about her," Mom said. "Especially after her illness."

"She's fine, Mom. Up and around. Walks with a cane but, outside of that, she's fine."

"Why in the world should she be walking with a cane?" Mom asked.

"Well, you don't get up and tap-dance after having a stroke," I replied. "But she has a golf cart, and she gets around pretty well."

"I don't understand," Mom persisted. "Helen was ill a number of years back, but not from a stroke. She had a nervous breakdown. I don't know what precipated it, but I heard your father discussing the case with Doctor Franchi."

"The head of Dale Vista?" I said, mentioning the name of our local sanitarium. "What did they have to say?"

"Nothing to me. Professional ethics. Just that it was

too bad, and she had a good chance for recovery. That's about all."

"Well, she's had a real run of bad luck," I said. "Because since then, she had a stroke."

"Oh. That's just awful for her. It seems that when things go wrong for people, it comes in bunches."

I told my mother that Harry wanted to stay over another night for the follow-up story and, barring any further complications, we would be sailing for home soon. She told me to be careful, brush my teeth, and call her when I knew more. I promised.

When I got back down to the saloon, the gin game was in full cry.

"Gin," said Captain Jack, laying down his cards. "And that's a blitz, Harry!"

"If Doris wasn't here, I'd tell you what you could do with your blitz, you pirate!" Harry exclaimed.

"You can tell him in a moment," I said. "I have something I want to check out."

"Something about the case?" Harry said, curious about anything that could be a story.

"Indirectly," I said. "I have to check out the Casino again. I saw something tonight. Or I think I did."

I felt a bit uneasy about lying to Harry. I wasn't going back to the Casino at all. But considering his involvement with Helen Grayson, I didn't want to go into it. Besides, there was a good chance I was dead wrong.

"Carl going with you?" Harry asked.

"No. He's questioning patrons at the Casino."

"Waste of time," Harry snorted. "No patron did it. You know as well as I do who's responsible. Satterfield." He scratched the side of his nose. "By the way, we should be leaving for the mainland tomorrow afternoon. If Carl is still speaking to me, I'll see you both at the hotel after breakfast."

"I think I know where you'll be for breakfast," I said. Harry smiled and gave me a wink. I said good-night to Captain Jack and set off down Main Street.

The lights were out in Helen Grayson's cottage when I got to the crest of Bison Drive. I wasn't disappointed. It wasn't necessary for me to see Helen. What I wanted to see wasn't inside the cottage itself anyway. I slipped around in back, and tried the door to the tool shed. It was unlocked. I eased the door open. It swung easily, on well-oiled hinges. I felt against the wall and located the light switch. For a second, the light from a high-watt, unshaded bulb that hung overhead blinded me. Then I began to search.

I'd remembered earlier how very clean the interior of the shed was. Too clean. I looked around under the bench. Not there. I found it in a corner of the shed. A large plastic trash can. I gave the lid a twist and peeked inside. It was there all right. Sawdust! I heard a sound behind me and I spun around.

There in the doorway, with her left hand propping her up, was Helen Grayson. In her right hand, she held an old-fashioned but very lethal looking revolver.

"Oh dear, Doris," she said. "I'm so terribly sorry you found that!"

10/Gracie Dawn

Mrs. Grayson marched me inside the house at gunpoint. I momentarily considered trying to disarm her. From the looks of the revolver she held, which seemed to be of Civil War vintage, there might have been a chance that it wasn't even loaded. But then again, one reads in newspapers all the time of people being accidentally killed by "unloaded" guns. I decided to play for time.

"I don't understand, Helen," I said, as she motioned me toward a door in the living room. "Why the gun? You know I'm no housebreaker."

"Don't play the innocent," she said with surprising venom. "Open the door. And if you move a hair, you get an extra eye!"

I did as directed and discovered that the door didn't lead to another room. It was a closet. "Inside, kid," she said. I entered the closet, she closed the door behind me, and I heard a lock click. I searched in vain for a closet light.

I must have been in there close to an hour. I'm not in the least claustrophobic, thank goodness. I had time to reflect on the jumbled events of the past two days. I knew now that Helen was heavily involved in the sabotage at the Casino, if not actually "the spook" herself. But how was she doing it? On the night the reflector ball fell, Harry Grubb had her golf cart. There was no conceivable way she could have traversed the town, done the deed, and walked back to her cottage.

She couldn't have committed the sabotage earlier in the day. The maintenance man, Slim, had told us the ball was tested in the afternoon, before the Casino opened its doors. She had to have an accomplice. Or *she* was the accomplice. But then, who could the "spook" be?

True, no one knew her whereabouts when the fire alarm went off. Harry said that he'd left her in the early afternoon. And at that time, Carl and Sparky Satterfield were combing the building, looking for clues. The only person I could come up with was Charlie Arthur. Even that seemed unlikely. His little museum was dependent on the tourist trade and, as he pointed out, what hurts the Casino hurts the island. It was also beginning to hurt my head.

But motivation was the last thing I should be worrying about, I told myself. There's a woman with a gun in the next room. No one knows that I'm here. I told Harry that I was going back to the Casino. I didn't tell Carl where I was going at all. My situation didn't look too promising. I could think of only one plan to disarm Helen Grayson when she opened the door to my closet.

In the dark, I looked for some sort of large garment,

or a blanket. I planned to throw it over her, if I had the chance. But when you're in total darkness, it's very difficult to figure out what's what. To complicate matters, there didn't seem to be any garments at all inside my impromptu prison. Just a number of cartons and hard-edged objects. I put my hand inside a carton and found something. It felt like an Indian club. You know, one of those heavy wooden bottle-shaped thingies that jugglers toss on T.V. I wasn't sure that's what it was in the dark. But I got a firm grip on the narrow end. I had a weapon. Just as I stood up and faced the door, the lock clicked.

"Come out with your hands on top of your head," Helen said through the door. "It's unlocked now." My heart sank. I set the thingie down and did as I was told.

I nearly fell through the floor when I saw who was waiting when I emerged from the closet. Or perhaps I should say *what* was waiting. Certainly the bizarre figure that greeted me in no way resembled Helen Grayson!

She wore a blond wig, in a style I'd only seen in old movies. The kind with cemented waves called a marcel. A gown that, oddly enough, looked almost in style —white satin with spaghetti straps at the shoulders above a perfectly acceptable neckline. Her mouth was a slash of red and her eyebrows two penciled arcs of perpetual surprise.

"It *was* you in the picture!" I blurted out.

"What picture?" she said, waving the pistol in a casual fashion. "I've posed for so many."

"In the lobby of the Casino," I said. "The picture of the Evylyn Phillips Band. I thought the woman at the piano looked like you, but I wasn't sure."

"It was me all right," she said. "The band was as square as a two-bit haircut, though. Namby-pamby ladies playing namby-pamby crap. It wasn't a band. It was a crowd." She made her mouth into a carmine expression of scorn. "And Evylyn was the biggest joke of all. You know that dumb broad couldn't play any instrument at all?"

"I never heard the band," I said.

"You didn't miss a thing, honey," she said with a toss of her coif. "Except for Ina Ray Hutton's Band, women's groups didn't swing. That's why I left."

"I thought you only played classical music," I said.

"She only played classical music," said the apparition in white satin, indicating a silver-framed picture of a young Helen Grayson on the Steinway.

"But that's you!" I protested.

"Bushwah," said the woman. "That's Helen Grayson. What a twerp! I'm Gracie Dawn. Jazz singer. Swing pianist. Arranger."

I began to realize what I was dealing with. If I was correct, the woman I was talking to actually believed that she was a separate person from Helen Grayson. I've seen films and read books that had characters with split personalities but, as with so many things you know exist in theory, you're always stunned when you actually encounter them. Like the tourist who couldn't get over the idea that Niagara Falls ran all night too. I took a chance and played along.

"But where is Helen Grayson?" I asked.

"Who knows?" she shrugged. "And who cares?"

"I'm sure that she'll be missed."

"Not by me, kid. I got things to do. I got a show tonight."

"Oh really?" I lied. "I'd sure like to see your show."

"Say, you don't have to worry, kiddo," she said. "You got a ringside seat for this one."

"How nice," I said, not feeling at all nice. "Where?"

"Are you kiddin'?" she laughed. "At the Casino of course. We're going to have the last real show at the Casino. When I get done, they'll be laying in the aisles. Except there won't be no aisles left to lay in!" She broke into a peal of hysterical laughter. I managed a sickly smile, although I had only the vaguest idea what she was talking about. Maybe if I could keep her talking to me. . . .

"I don't understand why you dislike Helen Grayson so much," I said softly. "Everyone else seems to think she's a marvelous person."

"She's all right. But she's a dummy. A sucker."

"How so?"

"Siddown, kid," she said, waving the horse pistol at the Morris chair. "I'm gonna tell you just how dumb that simple broad is."

I took the indicated chair. "Gracie Dawn" sat at the piano. I noticed that, when she walked, she hardly limped at all. "Gracie" set the pistol down within easy reach and opened a pack of Camels which she took from a silver mesh bag that lay atop the Steinway. She lit a cigarette with a silver lighter and blew a long stream of smoke at the ceiling. She began to speak in her brassy style.

"In 1940, when Helen was nineteen, she was a goody-two-shoes. Never said boo to a bug. Used to go to the mainland once a week for lessons, then come back to the island and practice. Five, six hours a day. All long-hair stuff. Then one night, when her folks were off the island, she did something they never let her do. She went down to the Casino to hear a big band. It was Artie Shaw. The dummy never heard any real heavy swing before that. Just Bach preludes and fugues, Chopin études. Like that.

"It messed with her head. Instead of going to her regular piano lessons, she started going to jazz places in Long Beach, then in L.A. After a while, she even stopped her classical lessons. After ten years of study. She went to a guy who taught jazz piano."

"What did her parents think of all this?" I asked.

"Hah! They didn't even know. They were too busy with their big house, their yacht, and the ritzy crap. Helen studied till 1940. The kid had a little talent. All that classical crap gave her good hands. She caught on."

"That doesn't sound like a stupid person."

"Oh, at music she was a whip. But when it came to people, she didn't have the sense God gave a gnat!" "Gracie" gave a short, barking laugh. "See, she thought she could play jazz with name bands. Couldja die laughing?"

"I don't understand."

"Neither did she, tootsie-face. Neither did she. Do you know the dumb broad actually tried to audition for big-name bands?"

"What's wrong with that?"

"You know?" "Gracie" said, cocking her head like a marcelled poodle. "You're as dumb as she was! For your information, women didn't play in men's bands. They didn't play jazz. They played all that square crap for crooners to sing. Except for Ina Ray and a couple of other groups, a women's band was for decoration. The music was an innocent bystander." She savagely ground out the Camel in a tray on the piano.

"She got a job, all right. With Evylyn Phillips. Didn't matter that she could play rings around anyone in the band. Evylyn wouldn't even give poor Helen a feature spot. Not one tune. See, there was only one star in the Phillips band. That was Evy-baby herself. And she couldn't blow her nose on pitch. So Helen, the poor dumbbell, she decided to audition for men's bands that cooked with gas."

"What happened?"

"Nothing, natch. She'd wait until any big-name band played at the Casino, then try to get someone to listen to her." "Gracie's" face took on a bitter expression. "They wouldn't even listen! They wouldn't even give the broad a chance!"

"How terribly unfair!" I said. "Just because she was a woman?"

"You got it, sister. Only one band leader listened. Jack Jameson."

"But he wouldn't give her a job either?"

"Oh, he was slick, Jack was. Listened to her. Told her she was just what he was looking for. He wanted to change the band's image. To have a good-looking woman play piano would make 'em flock to the Casino and the Palladium, he said."

"What happened then?"

"What do you think? Jack wasn't interested in Helen's talent, honey. At least not the kind that involved the piano. He only wanted to get her into the hay. And he sure did. Right under the Casino, in one of those little private rooms they had for stars' dressing rooms back then. Oh, boy, did he audition her. For every day in a four-week booking!" "Gracie" lit another Camel.

"And then came the day. The four-week booking Jack had at the Casino came to an end." "Gracie's" face softened. "Meet me at the marina, he told her. We'll be together. I've given my piano player his two weeks' notice, he said. Now don't forget . . . nine o'clock tomorrow morning . . ."

I could see that she was working herself into a rage. Perhaps I already knew what she was going to say. But I was fascinated by her story.

"And so you went to the marina at nine?"

"And he had sailed at seven. Didn't leave a note. Didn't leave anything but the baby that poor, simple Helen was carrying inside her."

"What did you . . . er, Helen do?"

"That's where the kid was so stupid. She told her parents. They could only think of one thing. The scandal and the blot on the precious family name. They shipped the poor kid off to an aunt in Illinois, where she had the baby. Then they put the baby up for adoption."

"How sad," I said. "For both Helen and the baby."

"Helen was a sad case, honey. She wanted the kid. But how could she have supported it? Her folks wouldn't give her a dime. And she found out how far she could go as a woman jazz player—two floors lower than the Camelot Casino ballroom. She rented a cheap hotel room on the north side of Chicago. In Rogers

Park. It had all the furniture she needed. In those days, you could get a room with what they called a pullman kitchen. She paid the first month's rent and stuck her head in the oven. Then turned on the gas. That's when she met me. I stopped her."

"I see," I said, not seeing at all. "You were living in the same hotel?" I knew this was nonsense. The woman, whatever she called herself, was Helen Grayson.

"I saved her," "Gracie" said, nodding. "I taught her how to dress, how to use makeup. I read all about it in movie magazines. Got her a good bleach job on her hair. She kinda looked like Jean Harlow . . ." "Gracie" looked at me. "But you wouldn't remember Jean Harlow. She was a movie star long before your time. They called her the Blond Bombshell."

"I know who Jean Harlow was," I said. "I've seen her in movies on the late show."

"Well, that's who she reminded me of. And I put her wise. Got her a job in a place on the near north side. Giovanni's. All she hadda do was play piano and sing." "Gracie" gave another mirthless laugh. "And be nice to Giovanni. And maybe a few special friends. . . . Then, one day, she woke up in a sleazy hotel bed with a hangover and a broken jaw. A souvenir from one of Giovanni's 'special friends.' The guy's specialty was killing people and dropping them into Lake Michigan with cement shoes on."

"How terrible!"

"Just a taste of real life, sweetie-face," "Gracie" said shortly. "So poor Helen decided to go home to Santa Catarina. But her high-and-mighty family wouldn't take her back. Her mother had died. Her father claimed she died of the shame that Helen brought down on the family. Right up until the day he died, Helen's father wouldn't see her or speak to her."

"What an awful thing to do to his own daughter!"

"Yeah, well, the Grayson family was like that. I figured out what Helen could do and I told her. She followed my advice. Let her hair grow out to its real color. Bought some frumpy dresses and went to a little crappy burg in California called Santa Amelia. Taught piano to no-talent kids."

"Like me."

"Nah, honey. There was lots of them worse than you. But a lot of them better too. Your mother was one . . . she could play the "Étude in E" by Chopin so beautifully . . ."

I watched in fascination. Somehow the mention of my mother, a talented student, was bringing Helen Grayson back to the surface of the tortured personality that was "Gracie Dawn."

"Tell me about it," I urged.

"Nothing to tell. She quit studying, married someone," she said. In an instant, the "Gracie" personality took hold again. It was eerie to see and hear. Sort of like when you're driving out in a deserted area and get a radio station that goes in and out. Or when you tune the dial between stations and they play almost at the same time.

"But what about her baby?" I asked. "Helen's baby. Wouldn't the father do anything to help?"

"Hah! All Jack Jameson was ever interested in was Jack Jameson. Stupid Helen wrote to him. He wouldn't even answer. The baby was adopted. And don't you know that Helen spent years trying to find the kid? She . . ." "Gracie Dawn" put a hand to her face, sliding out of phase again.

"I finally found her in Des Plaines, Illinois. She wouldn't see me. Said that so far as she was concerned, her mother was the woman who brought her up. And that for all she cared, I could butt out of her life forever. That was five, six years ago . . ." She stood up, barely having to lean on the piano for support. In that instant, Gracie Dawn returned.

"By then, all the Graysons were dead and gone. All but Helen. But her father was generous. He left her a little cottage. This one here. He left the big house, the money, all of it to charities. And Helen came back to live here."

"Well, at least her father left her *something.*"

"What did he leave her?" "Gracie" said bitterly. "A place where she could limp into town and see the big bands play at the Casino? Where all the crap started? A chance to see all the bands that turned her down come in and play to overflow crowds? Even the Jack Jameson Band! Oh, he wasn't alive anymore. Died in a car crash. . . . Hah! Even when he died, he still made people miserable. He was rotten drunk and killed a family of four on the Pasadena Freeway when his car jumped the divider. I laughed when I read he was dead. It should have happened years before it did, the lying bastard!" She was getting terribly upset, and that was the last thing I wanted. She reached down and picked up the old-fashioned pistol.

"But it's all over, baby," she snarled. "No more

watching the crowds come in. No more having the Casino standing there, always a reminder.... It taunts me. ... And it's all over. Tonight!"

She waved the gun at me. "Pick that up, and take it with you," she said, indicating a battered portable phonograph that lay in a corner.

"You're letting me go?" I said incredulously.

"Letting you go with me. And when I go, the Casino goes! Come on, out the front way!"

We took the golf cart. She had me work the simple controls, while she placed a suitcase almost the size of the phonograph behind us where, ordinarily, golf bags would be stowed. She directed me to a long side street at the foot of Bison Drive and had me turn left. I knew that there are a number of side streets in Camelot, but Main is the only one that runs uninterrupted through the town. I had hoped that we would take that route. But Helen/Gracie was an island native. We began a series of twists and turns, avoiding the one through street.

Not that we need have worried about being seen. The last mainland ferry had departed hours ago. Outside of the orangey lights of the streetlamps, all of the town was in darkness.

A sudden hopeful thought came to my mind. I had told Harry that I was going to the Casino. Perhaps Carl would still be there. Or maybe if he'd checked at my hotel room.... But hope died fast. The lobby lights of the Casino were dark. And I recalled how, last night, Carl had let me sleep in. He didn't even wake me the following morning. If I was to get out of this predicament, I was going to have to do it myself. And although she may not have been in her right mind, there was no doubt that her gun hand was steady as a rock.

"What are we going to do at the Casino?" I asked as we turned up the boardwalk.

"I don't know what you're going to do besides carry those two things for me," "Gracie" said. "But I'm going to blow that damned building to kingdom come!"

11/I'm Always Chasing Rainbows

"No, not the front way," "Gracie" said. "Around in back. By the delivery dock."

I took the turn she indicated and was soon at the freight dock. All deliveries to the Casino are made by boat from the mainland. There's a special pier and loading area. "Gracie" produced a flashlight from somewhere in the golf cart and snapped it on. We entered the place through two large, gray-painted doors which weren't even locked.

The interior of the loading area was illuminated by low-watt "trouble" lamps set in little wire cages overhead. We walked down a long corridor that yielded into the huge kitchens, also dimly lit. Finally we emerged through the swinging double doors that the waiters use and came into the darkened ballroom.

"On the stage," "Gracie" directed. "There's a doorway to the left."

We passed through the door and into the backstage area. There was a large array of switchboards, curtain ropes, and counterweights. "Gracie" knew her way perfectly. She went to one of the switchboards and flipped a control. From a high point on the back wall, a single bright spotlight flared into life, casting a circle of brilliant light onto the stage in front of the deserted bandstand. "Gracie" took a chair from behind one of the empty music stands and slid it toward me across the smooth stage boards.

"Have a seat, dearie," she said. "It's almost show time."

She went over to the grand piano and laid out the suitcase I had been carrying. When she opened it and began taking out the contents, my heart sank. I recognized the device that she was assembling. I'd seen one used when the Santa Amelia Civic Auditorium was built. It was an explosives detonator!

As she began twisting wires onto the terminals, she kept up a line of chatter. Like the driver of a tourist bus.

"The fools who run this joint have to be half-blind," she said. "I've been setting this up for years." She pulled on some wires from behind one of the big switchboards. "These leads go directly downstairs to the subbasement. Nobody questioned why they were there. Slim Carter doesn't know what half the equipment in the place is for anyhow."

"What are the wires connected to?" I asked, already guessing the answer.

"You name it, tootsie," she said. "Plastic explosives, dynamite, some old ammunition. It's a blaster's candy store down there."

"But how did you get it? Didn't anyone notice you bringing it onto the island?"

"Not a soul. On account of they were already here. The island was a military base during the war. They had three separate administrations: Coast Guard, Navy, and Marine Corps. One after another. Each group had ammo dumps and construction equipment. But with one thing or another, they never got around to removing the stuff when the war ended. The explosives got lost in the paper-work shuffle. There's still enough buried on the island to blow it out of the water. If you know where to look."

"But how did you know?"

"I didn't. Charlie Arthur did. He came across the first cache over two years ago. He was going to write it into that history of the island. I talked him out of it. Told him that people would be afraid to come to the island if they thought there was live ammunition in odd places." She giggled. "But no odder than under the Casino, where I've been planting them for a year and a half."

"But how? I mean your leg . . ."

"People always assume that a stroke is a permanent thing. That a person who's had one is useless for the rest of her life. It ain't so, honey. Sure, I'm not much good for dancing anymore. But I can walk all right. I can even play the piano, if it doesn't call for heavy classical pieces, or cut-time jazz."

"I wondered why the piano at your cottage was in tune. I played a scale, and it was in perfect tune. But I thought you had it done out of respect to the instrument."

"Partly, at first. But that's how I worked the knots out

of my left arm and hand. Started with the simple five-finger exercises for left hand. And I walked. God knows I walked all over the island. One by one, I found the places where the fireworks were stashed."

"But surely, someone saw you doing it?"

"Here? After dark? Honey, they take in the sidewalks after midnight. And in off-season, they don't even bother putting them out. If you don't want to see, or be seen on this island, it's easy. The year-round people are very private. That's why they live here to begin with."

"Gracie" finished hooking up the wiring she'd been working on as she talked. She came back from the switchboard with the detonator. With wires trailing behind her she set the deadly device on top of the grand piano that dominated the stage. She picked up the old pistol and laughed.

"Here," she said, tossing it at me. "I don't need it now. I got the machine and that's enough." She patted the side of the detonator. "Besides, the gun isn't loaded."

I quickly checked the heavy pistol. Empty. I could have kicked myself for not having made a try to escape earlier! But it's one thing to see somebody in a film disarm a person with a loaded gun. When it's real life and you're looking down a muzzle that seems the size of a canon, you don't take chances.

"Gracie" sat down at the piano and looked over at me. She ran her fingers over the keys. A clean but halting scale emerged. "Not too good," she said aloud, though I knew she wasn't speaking to me. "All this fetch and carry makes the hand weak for a while. Let's have some music, honey. Open up the record player.

There's already a record on the thing. But wind it up first. The crank is inside the top lid."

I did as I was told. I inserted the crank in its receptacle on the side and cranked it until it wouldn't turn any further. I checked the record. It was an old-time seventy-eight r.p.m. with an ornate blue-and-silver label. It was the Jack Jameson Band playing their theme, "Deep In a Dream."

"Go ahead, start it up," "Gracie" said. "It's going to be the last time the Jameson group plays the Casino. The last time *any* group plays here. Because when it ends, so does this place." She patted the detonator.

I knew she meant it. How she ever got this far, mining the foundations of the Casino, I couldn't imagine. But speculating on the how of it wasn't really on my mind. I had just one chance. If I stalled for time long enough, somebody might miss me. But then I thought of the "Queen's Messenger."

The phrase comes from the musical *The Threepenny Opera*, by Kurt Weill and Bertolt Brecht. It says, in effect, that if you are looking at the last minute for a message from the Queen to spare your life, don't bother. Because that only happens in shows. In real life, the Queen's Messenger never comes. I had to do something. But what? If I made a move for the detonator, she would just twist the handle, and boom. I got an idea.

"Gracie, why should Jack Jameson's Band be the last to play at the Casino? I've never heard you sing. I've only heard you . . . er, Helen, play classical music. Why shouldn't Gracie Dawn be the final act?"

Her expression softened. "You're right, sweetie. Absolutely right." She ran her fingers over the piano keys.

"What do you want to hear? Oh, I forgot. All my stuff is from before your time." She gazed at the ceiling reflectively. "I can't do any real up-tempo stuff. The hand won't work that good. How about a nice ballad?"

She played an introductory few measures and in a surprisingly lovely voice, began to sing:

> *I'm always chasing rainbows.*
> *Watching clouds drifting by.*
> *My dreams are just like all my schemes.*
> *Ending in the sky.*

I listened in fascination. After the first few bars, her voice became stronger. The old tune took on a new meaning. Each word she sang was evocative of a deep personal feeling.

> *Some girls can search and find the sunshine.*
> *I search and only find the rain.*

The poignant lyric reached me. All her life, Helen Grayson had chased a rainbow. She wanted to be a woman recognized for her talent and not for her beauty. She had tried to invade a man's world, and that invasion had turned out a disaster.

> *Some girls can make a winning sometime.*
> *I never seem to make a gain, believe me . . .*

In my mind's eye, the shape of "Gracie Dawn" began to change. As she sang in her remarkable voice, I could see the years drop away. She was in total command of her musical instrument and vocal equipment. She radiated poise and confidence. Perhaps it was the ghostly quality of the great, empty ballroom, but I could *feel* the presence of all the audiences that had laughed, drunk, dined, and danced here. The silence of the room was not the hush of an abandoned place. It was as though there was a full house keeping very, very still, so as not to miss a single note of her song.

I'm always chasing rainbows,
Waiting to find a little bluebird, in vain.

As she sang the last notes of the ballad, "Gracie" stopped playing the piano. She stood up and slowly raised her arms above her head. The time-honored signal to an audience that a singer has finished. If you have ever been fortunate enough to hear a truly great performance, you may have experienced the momentary hush that comes over an audience when the last note is sung. As a gesture of respect, there is a moment of silence that allows the last note to fade away. Then the roar of approval comes.

Despite the horrifying circumstances, "Gracie Dawn" had made me forget everything but her performance. I jumped to my feet and I applauded as I never have in my life. "Gracie" made an elegant bow. She acknowledged applause from all sides of the house, though I was the only one there. Perhaps she heard handclaps that I could not. Then I saw her hand move for the detonator.

"Wait!" I cried. "Not yet. A show isn't one song, Gracie. I want to hear more." Her hand hesitated. Although I felt a bit silly, I began to chant, as though there were hundreds of people present. "More! More! We want more!" She moved away from the detonator and came downstage and addressed her "audience."

"Oh, thank you, ladies and gentlemen. Thank you so much. You're all so wonderful. What can I say?"

"Don't say," I said like a cheerleader. "Sing. Play! We want more! We want more!"

"Gracie" returned to the piano with a radiant smile on her lips. She sat and began to play and sing once more. With each measure of the music, her piano playing became defter, more certain. Her voice soared. And there in the half darkness of the empty ballroom, I was afforded a rare experience. I heard "Gracie Dawn" in her first starring appearance at the Camelot Casino Ballroom.

The craziest part of it all was that when she'd finish another number and I applauded for all I was worth, I wasn't humoring a madwoman. "Gracie" was one of the best singer/players I have heard. Her repertoire was extensive and, unerringly, she chose the right sequence of songs. Lovely ballads by the Gershwins, Richard Rodgers, and Harold Arlen. Swinging show tunes by Cole Porter. Jazz standards by Duke Ellington. Finally, her last number was, of all things, "Someday My Prince Will Come" from Walt Disney's film *Snow White.*

As I listened, slow tears began to run down my cheeks. Her poor prince had never come. The man she thought was her prince turned out to be a self-serving knave. Her life had been one heartache after another. Yet, at that moment of song, the message of hope that someday a handsome prince would magically appear, and make things right, rang true. I held my breath as she negotiated the high note at the end. I needn't have worried. She was superb.

I leaped to my feet, applauding. "Marvelous!" I shouted. "Just wonderful!" I approached her and took my chance. "Oh, Miss Dawn," I said like a gaga groupie in front of a rock star, "may I have your autograph?"

She gave me a warm smile and said sweetly, "But, of

course, Doris, dear. I'd be delighted. But I don't seem to have a pen or paper here . . ." She looked around her, as though suddenly discovering her surroundings. Then she sat down heavily at the piano. She passed a hand over her face and then looked in surprise at the red smear of lipstick that marked it. "But what are we doing here at the ballroom?"

I'm sure that my sigh of relief was heard on the mainland. The woman at the piano was no longer Gracie Dawn. She was Helen Grayson. Perhaps realizing her lifelong ambition to star at the Casino had brought her back to sanity. I couldn't say. But I took no chances. I moved between her and the detonator atop the piano. She neither noticed nor seemed to care.

"You sang and played beautifully, Helen. I was amazed that you haven't played here as a star long before now."

"Oh, do you really think so, Doris? It's been so long since I played to an audience. . . . I. . . . Excuse me, dear. . . . I'm afraid I don't feel very well." She stood up momentarily and then, as gently as folding old velvet, she sank silently to the floor.

Immediately, the ballroom was ablaze with light. I was about to rush to Helen Grayson's side, when I suddenly realized that neither of us had touched a switch. I looked out into the ballroom and saw Carl Suzuki running across the dance floor toward the stage. On his heels was Sparky Satterfield, with Harry Grubb bringing up the rear. My knees weakened and I almost fell. Then I got hold of myself. As Carl vaulted up to the stage, I'm afraid that my first words were, "How long have you been here?"

"Caught the last part of the concert," Carl said, taking me in his arms. "You were brilliant, Doris. You handled her perfectly."

I looked over to where Harry Grubb was bent over Helen Grayson's unconscious body. The sheriff was busy dismantling the detonator. I went over to Harry's side.

"How is she?"

"I'm no doctor. But I don't think she's had another stroke, if that's what you mean. I think it's just emotional exhaustion. Her pulse is regular. But don't stand there. Call the ambulance!"

* * *

It was another picture-postcard day at the Cortez Bay Yacht Club. We were seated around the big table on the stern of the Parvenu as Harry Grubb held forth on the subject of Helen Grayson.

"She'll be all right eventually," he said. "I spoke with Doctor Franchi today, and he's optimistic. Oddly enough, that last concert she did was highly therapeutic, or so says the good doctor."

"I can say it now," Carl said. "She was magnificent. I had no idea she had such talent. And at her age too."

"For your information, sir," Harry said gruffly, "I do not consider a woman of sixty years as old. Perhaps because I am almost twenty years her senior. However, talent doesn't diminish with years. It adapts and modifies. What time may take away in terms of youth and strength, it also compensates for with added technique . . . expertise."

"I didn't mean she wasn't worth listening to on any

terms," Carl said. "I meant that her voice was as strong and true as a woman half her age."

"Forgive me if I seem too down to earth," I said. "But what *is* going to happen to her? There's a big legal cloud hanging over her now."

"It could be a lot worse," Harry said. "Doctor Franchi will testify that she wasn't responsible for the acts of Gracie Dawn. He's been working with my lawyers for the past two days."

It hadn't surprised me that Harry Grubb was taking care of Helen Grayson's medical care, nor that he was paying for her legal expenses. I had seen them together, before the scarifying concert in the empty Casino ballroom. I think that, as much as Harry Grubb could care for anyone, he cared for Helen. The proof of it was that he hadn't filed his story with *The Register* about that frightening night. I know that Sparky Satterfield wasn't all that interested in seeing more publicity harmful to his professional reputation noised about in the papers. After all, the person responsible for the sabotage at the Casino had been under his nose all the time. And he had never suspected her. But I didn't want to introduce that topic of conversation. Our gathering was too happy this day.

Harry and Carl had gone through all the 'I-told-you-sos' after we had taken Helen to the mainland and entrusted her to Dr. Franchi at Dale Vista Sanitarium. Harry went so far as to admit that Carl was right and he was wrong about Sheriff Satterfield. And that's as close as Harry Grubb gets to apologizing to anyone.

"Any legal opinion on the outcome?" Carl asked.

"It's too early to tell," Harry said. "No doubt she's off

the hook for the vandalism. The woman who was hurt in the fire panic is out of danger now. It may simply be a question of an out-of-court settlement to induce her not to press criminal charges."

"You'd pay her to drop charges?" Carl said. "That's sort of shady dealing there, Harry."

"Crap!" Harry snapped. "You're a lawyer. It's done all the time, and you know it. My lawyers will point out that a criminal case will only see Helen acquitted on the basis of her mental health at the time. The injured woman won't see a dime from it. Helen's poorer than Job's turkey. All she owns is that cottage on the island. If they clam up and drop charges, I can make it worth their while. Everyone's happy." He stood up and looked out at the harbor which looked as though it had been cleaned and polished for today's occasion. His expression brightened.

"But I have a surprise for you," he grinned. "Lunch is ready."

Carl groaned. I wasn't ready for Ismael's cooking either.

"Uh, I'm not awfully hungry," I lied.

"Don't cheat yourself of a rare pleasure," Harry said. He called out loudly, "Marcel!"

"Oui, monsieur?" came a voice from the galley.

"You may serve lunch now."

A tall thin man in his fifties, wearing chef's whites, came up from the galley and began serving a number of covered dishes. The aroma woke Petunia, who grunted ecstatically.

"Voilà, M'sieur Groob," he said, raising the covers of the dishes one by one. *"Coquilles St. Jacques,* lobster

thermidor . . ." He continued his recitation, each new dish a delight. He served us with great *éclat* and, after bowing deeply to all of us, disappeared into the galley again. I tasted the lobster thermidor. It was exquisite!

"I don't understand," I said. "What happened to Ismael?"

"He quit me," Harry said, grinning broadly. "And I couldn't be happier. Not just for the good of my stomach, but I got revenge on Captain Jack!"

"How so?"

"Well, it seems that every time Jack cleaned me at gin rummy, he was playing this game with Ismael. It goes like this." He held up a long, bony hand. "You keep your hand behind your back, like so. Then, on a count of three, you extend your hand. In a fist like this." He demonstrated. "Or two fingers, like this. Or palm up, like this."

"What does it mean?" I asked.

"It's all symbolic. The fist stands for a stone. The two fingers for scissors." He moved his two fingers together and apart to illustrate. "And the open palm symbolizes a piece of paper. You win or lose according to what the other guy shows on the three count. If you show a fist, and the other guy tosses two fingers, that means you win. Scissors can't cut a stone, you see?"

"What happens if you make a fist, and the other man makes a paper?"

"He wins. Paper envelopes the stone."

"I get it. And scissors would cut paper."

"Exactly."

"And Ismael won all the money from Jack that you lost at gin?" Carl asked. Then he began to laugh.

"I don't find losing money that amusing. Even secondhand losses," Harry drawled. "I only draw consolation from the fact that Jack got taken to the cleaners worse than he took me."

"Sorry, Harry," Carl said, still laughing. "I don't know if I should clue you in on why I'm laughing though."

"Tell me," I said. "If Harry doesn't want to listen, he can plug his ears." I knew what I was saying. Harry's such a snoop, he wouldn't have rested until he had found out. Carl collected himself and said, "It's an old Japanese game. Kids play it for fun. Adults gamble on it, because you can psyche out an opponent. It's really a game of skill and psychology."

"Okay, you know the game," Harry said crossly. "Why all the merriment at my expense?"

"I hate to tell you, Harry, but I taught the game to Ismael last weekend!"

"You *what?*" roared Harry Grubb.

"Sorry, old man, but it's true. Doris was sleeping late at the hotel. You were having breakfast with Helen Grayson. I had nothing much to do, so Ismael and I passed the time with the game. Once I taught him, that is. He picked it up real fast."

"He sure as hell did," Harry said reflectively. "He sure did."

A sly gleam came into Harry Grubb's eye. He began to chuckle to himself.

"You're taking it better than I expected," Carl said.

"Oh, I'll have my revenge," Harry promised. "You see, you don't know what Ismael did with all the money he won from Captain Jack. He's opening a Mexican restaurant!"

"My Lord!" I exclaimed. "Where?"

"That's where my revenge comes in," said Harry Grubb in triumph. "I won't tell you where it is. One day, unsuspecting, you'll go into Ismael's restaurant. Then you'll get what you deserve!" He laughed loud and long. "It's sort of a gastronomic Russian roulette!"

After lunch, Carl and I walked down the boardwalk that led to the clubhouse of the Cortez Bay Yacht Club. We held hands as we walked. He gave my hand a bit of a squeeze.

"Happy?" he asked.

"Yes and no," I admitted. "I still think of Helen Grayson. What a tragic life. I think what sent her around the bend was when her daughter wouldn't even see her. She's had enough heartbreak for two lifetimes."

"Well, even though it took a near tragedy to do it, I think she'll be happier now," Carl said. "Her prince finally did come, like in her song. True, Harry doesn't look much like a prince charming, but he surely does love her. You'd have to be blind not to see it."

"I suppose you're right," I admitted. "But a lot of what happened to her wasn't her fault. It was the time she lived in, and trying to crash a barrier that women are only beginning to break through now. Sexual discrimination."

"That, I won't go into," Carl said. "But now that I finally have you to myself for a few minutes, I want to talk."

"We are talking, Carl."

"Don't stall me, Doris. You've been doing that all weekend. You know what I was going to say, don't you?"

"I think so."

"Let me spell it out, then," Carl said, stopping our stroll. He put his hands on my shoulders and looked me straight in the eye. "I love you, Doris Fein," he said. "I have never known a woman quite like you. Oh, I know that there's almost twelve years between us. But there's twenty between Harry and Helen. I may not be a millionaire, Doris. But I have my ticket to practice law now. I have a responsible job in New York as an assistant district attorney. I was serious when I told you that I'm going into politics. And you'd be a . . . perfect wife for a rising young legislator. You're capable of entertaining high-level people, and I know you'd be a great hostess."

"But Carl, I . . ."

"No, let me finish before you say anything. And beyond your help to my career, we work well together. I never realized just how much you meant to me until Saturday night, when you were in danger."

I listened to Carl's earnestness and the rest of his speech with a hollow feeling in the pit of my stomach. I knew now what I had to say.

"In New York, when you were grabbed by those terrorists, I knew you were very important to my life. What I didn't know then was how *you* felt about— Larry Small. That it wasn't a serious relationship on your part. After I thought things out for six months, I knew for sure. Then, when I almost lost you at the Casino . . ."

"I don't think that I was in that much danger," I said. "Once I realized the nature of Helen's illness. What you recognize, you can deal with."

"Doris, please let me finish. I've been trying to figure out exactly how to say this. If you sidetrack me now. . . . Oh, damn! I forgot where I was!"

"I believe you were telling me how wonderful I am. It didn't make me mad, either."

"Oh hell, Doris, I love you! I want you to be my wife and my partner. We laugh at the same things, we play the same games. If it comes to that, you're the only woman I've ever felt comfortable with on a dance floor. I'm a rotten dancer, and you make me feel like Astaire. You don't have to answer right away, you know. Take all the time you need."

I sighed deeply. Here was the first proposal of marriage I'd ever had. I thought back on the days when I was big as a house and spent my life dropping tearstains on the pages of poetry books. How desperately I wanted to be loved in those days! But so much had happened since what Elizabeth Browning called "my childhood griefs." I love Carl. I know that too.

I squared my shoulders and said, "I need more time than you're ready to give me, Carl. You see, I have a great deal more to learn. Not just at U.C.I. I mean about myself. I want to know what my limits are. I've only begun my life as an adult person. There are so many places I haven't been. People I haven't met. Carl, I'm not certain that journalism and literature will be my career. But, whatever my career ends up being, I know this: I will not be another Gracie Dawn, sitting alone in a cottage, always wondering what it would be like to star at the Casino Ballroom. I want my chance to be what I will. And I feel that marriage now would take the edge off that chance. As Sartre said, you can't be anything to another unless you are first something to yourself."

I saw the look of hurt on Carl's face and, darn it, I felt tears begin to fill my eyes. But what's the greater hurt? If the feeling between us couldn't survive honesty, it would be too fragile to last. I came closer to him and on impulse, kissed him soundly.

"Yes, I love you, Carl. I just can't marry anyone until I have proven myself to me. Can you please ask me your question again, when I graduate from U.C.I.? If nothing else, I owe that to my parents. And yes, to myself." I finished my speech, and then the tears did roll.

Carl took a handkerchief from the breast pocket of his suit and dabbed at my face.

"I won't say it doesn't hurt," he said softly. "But I do understand. I couldn't stand in the way of your goals, Doris." He laughed then. "I don't think anything or anyone could, if you have your mind made up. You're a very gritty lady." He put out his hand. "Friends?"

I took the hand and kissed his palm. "Friends," I agreed.

"How about dinner tonight, then?" he said with a smile. "I still have ten days' vacation left, and there's no one I'd rather spend it with."

"Dinner it is," I agreed. "But on one condition."

"What's that?"

"It can't be Mexican. Not until I find out where Ismael's restaurant is located!"

Laughing, we walked to the clubhouse.